BEWITCHED SHIFTER

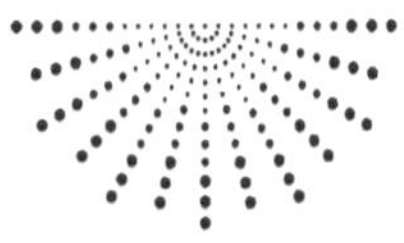

TAMSIN LEY

A Production of
Twin Leaf Press

*M*usic from the bar shook the sidewalk under Ashlyn's feet as she waited for the bouncer to check her ID. She'd let her new hair stylist talk her into "mermaid hair," and the pink and blue color seemed to make people think she was younger than her twenty-five years. That, and the fact that she was carrying cupcakes.

"They're mojito flavored," she told the bouncer, feeling stupid. *Who brings cupcakes to a bar?* "For a bachelorette party."

"Ah." The bouncer returned her card with a wink and waved her in. "They came in a while ago. Have fun."

"Thanks." She smiled and stepped inside. Since moving to Kenai a couple of months ago to take over her cousin's bakery, she'd come to appreciate how friendly the locals were. Even this bachelorette party was proof of that. Between baking and catching up on the mess cousin Lana had called bookkeeping, she'd barely had time to meet anyone. Muffy, a local bride-to-be, had come into the bakery looking for a quote on a wedding cake and, after learning Ashlyn was new in town, had invited her to the party.

Ashlyn wasn't usually one to take invitations from complete strangers, but she needed friends, and Muffy seemed nice. At least the party would get her out of the house.

Pausing just inside the door, she scanned the crowd for Muffy's familiar face. Multi-colored lights flashed over a tiny dance floor packed with people, and patrons hovered around high-topped tables nearby. A long bar extended through the center of the room, and the delicious aroma of fresh Alaskan halibut and steak fries drifted from the kitchen in the back. Her stomach growled. She'd been too busy for lunch today, and sugary cupcakes weren't going to cut it, especially if she was going to be drinking.

Laughter caught her attention from several semi-circular booths along the wall. A group of women in low-cut blouses held shot glasses in the air, and she spied Muffy's dark, artistically tousled tresses beneath a sparkly plastic tiara. Nerves tightened her belly. She wasn't shy, but joining a clique of women who already knew each other was always awkward. Too bad Cousin Lana was busy on her fishing boat or Ashlyn would've made her come along.

Straightening her shoulders, she headed over, looking at Muffy's white sash proclaiming her soon-to-be hitched status. *Cliché.* But she kind of liked cliché. It felt stable. Predictable.

The bride-to-be spotted her and rose, leaning across the table and waving her manicured pink fingertips in a shooing motion at her other friends. "Scoot over, let Ashlyn in. Ashlyn, this is Jen, my sister. She's visiting from Idaho. I'm trying to convince her she should move here." She pointed to the auburn-haired woman Ashlyn settled next to, then toward the other women at the table. "And these are my friends Bev, Christy, and Alison."

The women greeted her with smiles, and Ashlyn felt a warming welcome flow through her. She hadn't realized how much she missed hanging out with friends. She didn't know these ladies yet, but they seemed really nice, and the penis-themed gag gifts scattered across the table promised they had a sense of humor. *Maybe they'll even appreciate my bad jokes.* But first, she'd bribe them with cupcakes.

Ashlyn held out the pink pastry box. "I thought you might like some treats."

"Oh, you're so sweet. You shouldn't have!" Muffy set the box aside and pushed a shot glass at her. "Here, drink. You need to catch up!"

The sharp scent of tequila wafted from the glass. Last time she'd had tequila, she'd turned into a bitch and alienated everyone at the party. Not that Ryan, her ex, hadn't deserved every ounce of her alcohol-fueled anger, but she definitely could've handled the break up better. "No thanks. Really."

"Oh, come on! The bakery is closed tomorrow!" Muffy wiggled her shoulders in time to the music, gravity-defying breasts staying perfectly in place. "Live it up a little."

Ashlyn reached for the laminated menu buried beneath the gag gifts. "You do not want to see me on tequila. Besides, I haven't had dinner yet."

"We have appetizers on the way." Muffy splayed a hand over the menu, pressing it flat against the table. "Don't worry."

Jen leaned closer, auburn tresses cascading over bare shoulders. "Just do the one and she'll leave you alone."

"At least until the next time someone says you know what!" Bev—a blonde who Ashlyn thought might've been in the bakery a time or two—gave an exaggerated wink.

"What words are we not allowed to say?"

"Oh, she's sneaky!" Jen laughed. "Trying to trick us into saying them out loud."

"I told you you'd like her." Muffy leaned over to drape a string of Mardi gras beads over Ashlyn's head. "Jen made a list. It's somewhere in there." She gestured to the baubles strewn over the table. "But everyone has to do at least one shot to start."

Ashlyn was a lightweight, and any amount of

alcohol would go right to her head. On the other hand, a small buzz *would* help her relax. She tipped the shot glass back. The tequila burned an oily trail down her throat, followed by a moment of vertigo. *Whoa, that was fast.* She scrunched her eyes and shook her head. "Ack!"

"Yeah!" several of the ladies at the table cheered.

Ashlyn accepted a piece of paper titled BACHELORETTE BINGO as another round of shots arrived. The waitress set a glass in front of her and Ashlyn said, "Thank you."

That was apparently one of the things they weren't allowed to say, and the surrounding women started chanting, "Drink! Drink!"

Stomach twisting, Ashlyn looked over her shoulder, hoping for the promised appetizers. The waitress had moved to another table, but food had to be arriving soon, right? *You didn't come out tonight to be a party-pooper.* Taking a deep breath, she lifted the glass and downed it.

She knew right away she'd made a mistake. Stomach revolting, she shot to her feet. "Excuse me."

"Are you going to the bathroom? Wait for me," Muffy said.

Ashlyn didn't wait. The tequila was coming up, and she'd prefer not to spew all over her new friends. The bathrooms had to be near the back, right? She elbowed through the crowd of sweaty bodies to reach the rear of the bar. No bathrooms, only a door to the kitchen and an emergency exit. Tequila rising in her throat, she shoved against the exit door.

Blessedly cool night air flooded over her, and she only managed to stumble a few steps outside before she doubled over and heaved into the dirt alley. After a couple of spasms, her stomach was empty. She rested with her hands on her knees, panting. Glancing upward, she noticed the aurora borealis was out, ribbons of green light roiling behind wisps of clouds. This was the first time she'd seen the lights since moving here, and she wished she was in a better condition to enjoy them.

The alley remained quiet but for the muffled beat of the music from inside as she took a few deep breaths. Ugh, she hated throwing up. And the smell—it'd been gross out here before she'd barfed. Now it was disgusting. At least the door didn't appear to have been hooked to an alarm.

Straightening, she wiped her mouth against the back of her hand and turned to the bar. She collided into the solid chest of a man. *Fuck.* The bouncer must've come to check on her. She raised her chin. "Excuse me, I was…"

A pair of glowing purple eyes met hers.

She gasped and stumbled back. She'd heard of tequila giving people hallucinations, but she'd never had any herself.

The man opened his mouth, exposing unnaturally pointed teeth. She backed up another step. Her heart was about to pound its way out of her chest. His mop of hair had a white streak down the middle, and her mind immediately conjured images of Frankenstein's Bride.

Knowing it was a bad joke, but unable to stop herself, she murmured, "It's alive!"

In a move almost too quick to follow, he reached for her.

She screamed, trying to remember anything from the self-defense class she'd taken in high school. But that'd been almost ten years ago. Like claws, his fingertips jabbed into her arms, yanking her toward him. His face descended to her shoulder, and pain seared through her.

Did he just bite me?

Agony surged through her. Pain. Anger. Fury. Her entire being seemed to explode in a shower of sparks and fur. *Fur?* Her lips curled back from her teeth.

The next thing she knew, her mouth was against his throat. The taste of iron coated her tongue.

Not iron. Blood.

What the fuck was happening? She wasn't in control. Her head twisted, jaws refusing to let go. She felt the tear of flesh and heard an awful gurgling as the man's hands pawed uselessly against her. The light in his eyes shifted to green, and she swore he whispered, "Thank you."

Then the glow faded to darkness.

CHAPTER TWO

Kepler arrived on the scene as the nearby Orthodox church bell began chiming midnight. He climbed out of his Jeep and retrieved his forensics kit from the back. Red and blue police lights reflected off the bar's sheet metal roofing. Tourist season was nearly over, but a swarm of onlookers pressed against the police tape blocking the alley.

He pushed through the crowd, ignoring the irritated looks, and ducked under the police tape. The officer watching the line nodded as he passed.

Near the bar's dimly lit rear exit, blood darkened the packed dirt between the dumpsters. The air stank of bad seafood, vomit, and garbage. Kepler forced his shifter senses down, breathing shallowly as he took in the scene. A lanky man with curly hair sprawled on his back near the rear exit, throat torn open like a package of hamburger.

Kepler paused next to a bloody paw print the size of a melon. Bear attacks weren't unheard of in the town on the banks of a river known for its salmon runs, but this wasn't the print of a bear. It was a wolf, and a big one. *A shifter.* He knew that even without verifying the scent.

Near the bar's back door, Cal, the local police officer, broke from conversation with a State Trooper and strode over, broad freckled face unusually grim. Cal was also a wolf shifter and had been the one who'd contacted Kepler when the rogue outbreak showed up in Kenai. Both outsiders to the local pack, they'd become fast friends in the three months since Kepler'd transferred here.

Cal pulled a tube of vapor rub from the breast pocket of his police uniform and offered it to Kepler, speaking in a low voice. "Victim's a shifter. And he has those freaky white marks we've been looking for."

Kepler shook his head, declining the vapor rub. Much as he hated the scent of a crime scene, his nose often detected clues that might otherwise be overlooked. It helped him excel at his job, and he'd already earned grudging respect within the good ol' boys club that dominated the Major Crimes Unit. He bent to get a closer look at the body. "Any idea who took him out?"

"Nope." Cal shrugged. "We're telling the press it was

probably a bear attack. You think you can bring me in on this one?" Cal wanted to join the forensics unit, but lacked formal training, and Kepler didn't yet have the clout to get him a position with the human-dominated state law enforcement agency.

"I'll take it up with Finch, but you know how it is. We have to maintain jurisdiction. How's class going?" Kepler'd helped him sign up for an online course.

"I fucking hate homework," Cal complained. "Are you sure there isn't a way to test out?"

"The test won't use your shifter senses, Cal, you know that. It's all about chain of custody procedures, documentation—"

"Yeah, yeah, I know." Cal waved off the familiar lecture. "I've been studying. Go do your thing. I'll keep the humans occupied. Just let me know how I can help."

Nodding, Kepler pulled out his camera and started taking photos. The white streak definitely indicated the man had gone rogue, which meant that whoever had killed him was of secondary concern, at least to the shifter community. What or who was causing shifters to turn rogue was Kepler's primary mission. Back in Diablo Falls, the rogue outbreak had been blamed on a witch's hex, although that hadn't been proven before the outbreak ended. Steeling himself for an onslaught of sensory input, Kepler dragged in a breath, sniffing for clues. Blood. Garbage. Wolf shifter. *Mate.*

He shot to his feet and backed away. *Mate?* Not the

dead shifter, but the other wolf who'd been here. The one who'd most likely made the kill. Wildflower honey and musk. A scent that made his inner wolf come to attention and demand action.

He realized he was panting when Cal offered the vapor rub again. "Change your mind?"

"I'm fine." Kepler rubbed his palms against the front of his slacks uncomfortably. All shifters longed to find their perfect match, their destined mate, but this situation was about the least romantic he could've imagined. He didn't have time to deal with a mate, especially not one who was also a suspect. "You don't smell anything unusual, right?"

"No, why?"

The back door to the bar swung open and a young woman wearing a plastic tiara emerged, phone in hand. Cal turned, one hand up to stop her. "Hey, you can't be out here."

The woman looked at the body with wide eyes. "My friend is missing and I'm worried about her."

"Well, she's not out here." Cal hurried over and ushered the woman inside.

Kepler turned back to the crime scene, gaze following the bloody paw prints circling the body. They led toward the other end of the alley. His wolf was urging him forward. Yearning to meet this woman. His human mind kept a tight leash on the beast inside him. He couldn't let hormones cloud his investigation of the crime scene.

Heart thundering against his ribs, he walked down the alley, watching every footstep to be sure he wasn't missing any clues. The prints faded quickly, but the scent of honey and female grew stronger.

He froze at the corner of a dumpster, nostrils twitching. She was here. *Right here.* His hormones were screaming at him. He called softly, "Hello?"

From inside the dumpster came a soft, breathy sob.

Throat tight, he cracked open the lid. A pair of glowing blue eyes met his.

"Don't come any closer," a woman choked out.

He lifted the lid higher, exposing a naked, amber-skinned woman cowering in one corner of the container, surrounded by crushed takeout boxes and empty alcohol bottles. Flowing pink and blue hair tangled across her round, anguished face, the bright colors completely at odds with the grim surroundings. She seemed familiar, but he couldn't place her. She likely just felt familiar because his wolf insisted they were mates. "Are you okay?"

"I said stay back!" She bared her teeth, glowing blue eyes flashing. Drying blood marred her smooth skin, and her shoulder had a fresh crescent of puncture wounds.

He glanced down the alley toward the body, putting together the pieces. *That mother-fucking rogue attacked my mate.* His wolf was going crazy. *Protect her.* He extended his free hand toward her and spoke in his most soothing tone. "It's okay. I'm not going to hurt you. What's your name?"

Her delicate bare shoulders heaved with rapid breaths. "You don't understand. I killed him. Stay back."

Shit. Her wolf form must've taken over to defend her from her attacker. "It's not your fault. My name's Kepler. Detective Kepler Stone."

She stared at him a long moment, wariness fading from her eyes. "Detective Stone?"

"Yes." He leaned into the dumpster, hand still extended. She seemed to recognize him, but he'd met a lot of people since moving here and wasn't surprised. "Let's get you out of here before the humans start asking questions."

Wariness flared in her eyes again, and she shrank deeper into the corner. "Humans? What are you talking about?" She choked on a sob. "I don't know what's happening to me."

His blood turned to ice. Was she not a shifter? He inhaled deeply, sorting through the other smells to focus on hers. His wolf insisted she was both shifter and his mate. Definitely wolf. Something like ashes. Vomit. Perhaps she was suffering a form of post-traumatic stress amnesia. Every protective urge in his body surged to full strength.

Uncaring of who might be watching from the other end of the alley, he removed his shirt and held it toward her. "What's your name?"

"Ashlyn," she whispered. With a trembling hand, she accepted the shirt. "Ashlyn Reed. I run the bakery."

He blinked as understanding flooded over him. He'd stopped by the bakery a couple of times to pick up a dozen bear claws to share at the office. Why hadn't he scented her as his mate then? Hell, he hadn't even realized she was a shifter. None of this was making any sense. A human shouldn't be able to become a shifter without visiting the hidden glacial spring, and he doubted that's what'd happened here.

He glanced toward the bar's back entrance, where Cal and the Trooper were once more in conversation. The Trooper was human, and part of Cal's job was to keep him engaged while Kepler investigated. Most humans didn't know about shifters, and the Shifter Council wanted it kept that way. But what about Ashlyn?

She was choking back sobs and fumbling to put an arm in the shirt he'd given her. Her entire body trembled like leaves in a storm. Until he could figure this out, he needed to protect her. Protect his mate. "You've obviously had some shocking experiences tonight. Let me take you somewhere safe so we can talk, okay?"

With a shaky breath, she nodded and rose, giving him a glimpse of her naked body. The mating urge was strong, and he felt his body react, despite the sordid environment. *Rein it in*, he told himself, keeping his lips secured over his emerging fangs and his eyes cast down to hide their unearthly glow. The last thing Ashlyn needed was a horny mate she didn't even realize existed.

As her bare feet settled to the dirt, she looked up at him. "I—I'm not supposed to say thank you," she said with a hiccup, then started to laugh.

He had no idea what that meant, but she was obviously not in her right mind. He had to get her away from the scene and calmed down before asking questions. Before the Trooper or any other humans spotted her, he swept Ashlyn up in both arms. No way was he putting Ashlyn into human law enforcement custody. He could trust Cal to come up with an excuse for his disappearance.

Heading toward the far end of the building, he circled the parking lot toward his Jeep. Ashlyn clung to his neck, her wildflower honey scent laced with tequila, garbage, and the ozone-like odor of magic. *Does that mean she might be a rogue, too?* His steps faltered as he examined her pink and blue tresses in the light of the moon. No indication of a white spot.

Relieved, he buckled her into the passenger seat and jogged around to the driver's side. He started the engine and turned toward home. Once he had her safe, he could plan out their next steps.

Ashlyn remained silent as he drove, staring out the windshield and clutching the front of the shirt closed. He pulled into his driveway, grateful for the tall wooden fence between his yard and the neighbor's. As he turned off the Jeep, Ashlyn seemed to come to life. "Shouldn't you take me to the hospital?"

"Shifters don't need hospitals." The words were out before he thought them through.

"Shifters?" she whispered, eyes round. The smell of adrenaline flooded the Jeep.

He ran a hand over his hair. *Idiot*. He needed to be more subtle. She didn't know what she'd become. What her world was going to be like from now on. "You're going to be okay. I promise. Let's go inside so I can explain."

She blinked at him, as if tempted to believe him, then glanced out the window. "Where are we?"

"My house. You can clean up, then I'll answer all your questions."

Her eyes narrowed. "Why don't you take me to my house?"

"I can protect you better here." He let a thread of his Alpha power infiltrate his words, hoping to reassure her he could keep her safe and also to compel her to obey. He generally didn't use his power because it confused other shifters, making them think he was looking for a pack. Kepler preferred to run as a lone wolf, but now that he had found his mate, that was likely to change.

He opened his door and went around to open hers for her. Too late, he spotted the neighbor's chihuahua taking a crap on his lawn as it had every day since he'd moved in three months ago. The little fucker had a complex and was in rivalry with the "big dog" next door—aka Kepler's wolf. The chihuahua started barking.

With fluid dexterity, Ashlyn shifted into a gorgeous cream-colored wolf with an amber ruff. Canines bared, she leaped past him, lunging for the dog.

Kepler tackled her just before her jaws snapped over the smaller animal.

The chihuahua scurried around the fence, unharmed, but yipping in terror.

Twisting free, Ashlyn faced Kepler, front paws set wide. Then her wolf lifted her muzzle and howled, voice resonating with power.

His veins turned to ice. *She's a fucking Alpha?* She didn't even know what a shifter was, and her animal was an Alpha, the most difficult form to control. The ice became daggers through his heart.

His mate was in real trouble.

They both were.

CHAPTER THREE

Ashlyn's entire body vibrated in the aftermath of the howl, a song with meaning she didn't understand. She saw through the darkness with more than her eyes—the air smelled sharper and the sounds from nearby houses buzzed like static on a phone line. She hadn't been able to restrain the urge to put the yipping ankle-biter on the lawn in its place. To punish it. Dominate it.

Then Kepler had crushed her against the damp grass, and she lost interest in killing. Now she wanted something else. Something just as primal. His hard muscles, sexy golden eyes, and woodsy clean scent made her want to lick him all over. Good God, she wanted to shove her nose in his crotch!

Kepler shook his head as if dizzy and demanded, "Change back."

Power pulsed through his words, a heaviness that

made the hackles on her neck and shoulders rise. His golden eyes glowed with unearthly light. A violent desire to prove she would not be controlled swelled inside her, and her muscles coiled to lunge.

"I said shift," Kepler said again, more guttural this time, a sound she felt in her bones.

Grudgingly, her beast relinquished its hold. Ashlyn conformed back to her familiar human self, crouched on hands and knees against the cool, dewy grass, nighttime breeze caressing her bare skin. She was naked again, the shirt he'd given her scattered in pieces all over the lawn. For some reason, that didn't bother her now. It felt… natural. She blinked, staring down at her hands splayed on the damp grass. What the hell was happening to her?

To her surprise, Kepler dropped to his hands and knees, touching his nose to hers. Despite her confusion and terror, he seemed exponentially handsome right now. Rough stubble covered his chin, not quite a beard but perfectly trimmed in a way that made her think about how it would feel against her inner thighs. She licked her lips, tilting her chin to bring their mouths closer.

His breath fanned her face. "We have to go inside."

Next door, the neighbor's porch light came on, spilling light over the tall fence. She stiffened, remembering the chihuahua. "Did I hurt that dog?"

"It's fine. Come on." He rose, dragging her to her feet.

Numbly, she followed him onto the porch. He shielded her from the street with his body as he unlocked the door and ushered her inside a small kitchen with a breakfast nook.

Whatever adrenaline had kicked in earlier was fading fast, and her arms and legs began to tremble. He'd used a word—shifter—in reference to her situation. She would never have believed him if she hadn't just experienced the change a second time. *Am I possessed? Infected?* She was so confused.

Resting her weight on one hand against the counter, she breathed deeply and blinked, staring at an empty egg carton next to a sink holding a few dishes. She didn't want to cry, exactly, but her eyes felt watery. *Weak.*

Kepler put an arm around her waist, supporting her against him. "Come on. Once you're cleaned up, you'll feel better."

God, he felt so good. So normal. He guided her through a sparse living area to a bathroom with outdated fixtures and a hamper overflowing with laundry. Her skin reeked like garbage, blood, and sweat, but he was wearing a musky cologne that made her mouth water. Sex ought to be the last thing on her mind right now, but she couldn't help it. The scent was one that probably got him laid all the time.

The thought of him with another woman made the beast inside of her snarl and rise to the surface, but she used every ounce of willpower to keep it suppressed.

Kepler had helped her get it under control once, but that didn't mean he could do it again, no matter how distracting his cologne was. Plus, the last thing he'd want would be some chick he just pulled from a dumpster.

He picked up a stray sock from the floor and dropped it into the hamper before jamming the lid closed, then leaned into the tub and turned on the shower. He urged her toward the water with a hand at the small of her back. "There you go."

The only thing grounding her at the moment was his touch, and she couldn't force herself to step away. She stared at the running water as if hypnotized.

Heaving a deep breath, he toed out of his shoes and stepped into the shower, pulling her after him. "I've got you."

He yanked the plastic shower curtain closed, and she dimly noticed he hadn't removed his pants. But his chest was bare, and his skin against hers felt so good, so stable, so *human*. Facing him, she let the water sluice over her scalp and down her back.

He picked up a bottle of shampoo with his free hand and massaged a masculine smelling lather into her hair, his touch more gentle than she expected. Picking up a bar of soap, he rubbed it between his palms then carefully cleansed the tender bite on her shoulder. One at a time, he soaped her hands, taking care to lavish each finger with attention.

She closed her eyes and let him. Although his touch

wasn't intentionally sexual, his warm masculine presence permeated the small space, and a heat was growing between her legs. His fingertips smoothed the grime from her cheeks and chin. The broad pad of his thumb brushed her lips. On instinct, she opened her mouth, flicking her tongue against his wet skin.

He exhaled sharply before pulling free. "Don't let her control you."

Is he talking to himself? She opened her eyes, but he turned her around with firm hands and smoothed soapy palms down her back to the top of her buttocks. His thumbs brushed the base of her spine, fingers circling around her hips, then he rubbed down the outsides of her legs. Despite his avoidance of any erogenous zones, the pressure of his touch ignited her desire. In fact, his careful evasion only made her want him more. She had no idea what was wrong with her, but she'd lost control. The funny thing was that she didn't care.

She placed both palms flat on the tiled wall in front of her and arched her back. Behind her, his breathing roughened. She waited, abdomen tightening as she anticipated his next move.

Slowly, his hands made a return path up the backs of her legs, bypassing her ass to return to her back. "You're making this difficult," he grated.

A primal urge she didn't understand rumbled through her body like thunder. Backing up a step, she rubbed her ass against him. The impressive length of his arousal pulsed hotly through his pants. She moaned. God, he felt so big. So ready. She slid a hand down between her thighs, finding her folds already slick. Her finger slid between them easily, gliding over the sensitive bud. She rocked into him in time with her finger.

A low groan escaped him and his hands dug into her hips. "Stop."

"I need you." Had she just said that? She'd thought Detective Kepler Stone was sexy from the first time he'd walked into the bakery, but she wasn't usually this brazen. After the night she'd had, however, nothing could surprise her. Imagining him slamming into her was a much better thing to focus on than the other things that had happened.

He leaned forward, hard abs against her back, and cupped her breasts. Her nipples sharpened to aching points. She rubbed herself harder, the pressure inside her building. Even so, her own touch wasn't going to be enough. She needed filled. She needed Kepler.

Turning in his embrace, she reached for his belt, struggling with the water-logged leather. She hadn't been with a lot of guys, and she'd definitely never been this close to one with an honest to God eight-pack. The bulge in his pants promised it would live up to the rest of his body. His fingers encircled her wrists and pulled her hands up his strong chest to embrace the back of his neck. Pressing his forehead to hers, he met her gaze, the gold glow in his eyes hungry. Voice gravelly with desperation, he whispered, "You need to slow down. This means more than you realize."

She didn't know why, but she wanted to cry. Her loneliness since moving to Kenai faded, and in this moment, she had the distinct feeling she would never be lonely again. This moment was important. *Connected.* She angled her face until their lips brushed. "I want to be with you."

Kepler inhaled deeply, chest swelling against her naked breasts, and his hands fell to her hips. He leaned in, claiming the kiss she offered. She slid one hand from behind his neck and cupped his cheek, his whiskers rough against her palm as their lips explored each other. God, he was good, the perfect balance between gentle and firm, and she felt clumsy compared to him. He sucked gently on her top lip, pivoting them under the spray until her back rested against the tiled wall.

She lifted one leg, hooking it over his hip, and he leaned in, rolling the hard line beneath his fly against her center. She moaned against his mouth. Kepler pushed his tongue between her lips, dipping shallowly past her teeth. Ashlyn gasped and tilted her head, accepting his entry. He plunged his tongue deeper and harder, each stroke of his tongue mimicked by a gentle roll of his hips. Crushing her against the tile, he kissed her into senselessness, his erotic movements turning her insides to liquid heat.

His hand slid between her thighs. When he found

her waiting heat, he buried his face against her neck, nibbling along the edge of her throat in a way that made her gasp.

Tilting into his touch, she clutched the bulging muscles of his shoulders while he worked her. His expertise made her dizzy as he ran his touch along her slick folds. One finger dipped inside her and her inner walls clenched around him. He growled and sucked hard on her neck. He'd probably made a bruise, but she liked it.

She hung on while he pushed in and out of her with his finger, drawing her toward climax. She was close. Frustratingly close. But she needed more.

She reached for his belt again. "I want you inside me."

This time, he didn't stop her. He pulled back enough to let her fumble with his buckle, his fingers continuing the aching rhythm that left her gasping for breath. By the time she had him free, her eyes were rolling back with pleasure. Still, she was determined to take this all the way. Take *him* all the way. She wrapped her fingers around his searing shaft and guided the head to her entrance. The man was enormous, pulsing and thick and hot.

Kepler exhaled, and she looked up to find his eyes on hers. The glow behind them was like a furnace, its flames ready to consume her. He bared his teeth and grated, "I can't stop."

"I don't want you to."

One large hand slid up the back of her thigh, lifting her against him. Wrapping her other leg behind him, she locked her ankles. With a snarl, he slid into her. His girth filled her, stretched her. So big. Almost too much, but it felt amazing to finally have him inside her. He held there, pinning her against the tiles, buried deep inside her. Her hands clawed into his shoulders, and her insides fluttered around him on the verge of ecstasy. She threw her head back and moaned, "More."

Easing out slowly, he adjusted his grip under her ass and brought his chest against hers, leaning forward to claim her lips. His tongue plunged into her mouth in time with his next stroke. She tightened both legs around his hips, drawing him deep. His next stroke was harder. Faster. Surer. Then he was driving into her, pressing her back against the cool tiles, his mouth moving along her throat, stubble rough against her sensitive skin as he nipped and sucked. She braced her shoulder blades against the wall, finding it hard to breathe against the pressure of her building climax.

She exploded with blinding intensity and screamed his name, shuddering with the contractions of her inner walls. He slammed deep inside her again, snarling as she tightened around his thick shaft. His sudden release filled her with jets of warmth, his body bucking and shuddering against her. Her fluttering aftershocks almost made her pass out. Against her shoulder, she felt the light pressure of his teeth.

She thought of other teeth. Another bite she'd

experienced only a short while ago. Yet Kepler's teeth didn't frighten her. He made her feel safe. Protected. She wanted—needed—him to bite her. She slid her hand to the back of his head and drew him closer. "Do it."

Kepler's jaw clenched, the pressure of his teeth insanely close to piercing her skin. It hurt, but she wanted it to. She wanted him to cover the horrible experience in the alley with a better memory. "Please, Kepler."

"No," he said under his breath, then louder, "No!"

With a suddenness that felt like a vacuum, he broke contact.

She stumbled as her feet hit the tub basin. He had stepped out of the tub and was backing into the corner between the sink and the wall. His features were dissolving in a shower of sparks.

"Get out!" he roared. Then his voice lowered to a long, echoing howl.

CHAPTER FOUR

For the first time in years, Kepler lost control to his wolf. As his body transformed, Ashlyn's face paled. She scrambled toward the edge of the tub, one hand grasping the shower curtain for support. The plastic tore free, sending her crashing to the bathroom floor, half in and half out of the tub.

I shouldn't have given in to her advances. Should've maintained control of his wolf's urges. But Ashlyn had been so damned hot, so willing, so *wet.* He'd told himself he'd only go far enough to please her. But now his wolf was demanding more. He wanted to *claim* her. To cover the scar that bastard rogue shifter had put on her shoulder. To bind her to him as his mate. He should've taken her to the pack right away, not tried to protect her himself. He was too close to the situation to remain objective. But all he could think at the moment was: *Mine.*

The running shower splashed down Ashlyn's back and puddled onto the linoleum, a haze of shifter magic swirling across her beautiful amber skin.

Don't shift, don't shift, he begged her in his mind. His wolf pricked his ears, tongue lolling in anticipation. If Ashlyn shifted, they'd probably both lose control and run through the streets in a mating frenzy, hunting chihuahuas together. His wolf thought that sounded fun. Kepler chomped down on his own tongue, tasting blood. *Not fun. Deadly,* he reprimanded, hoping the potential danger to his mate might force his beast to relinquish control. Not only was she a newly turned shifter—which should be impossible without visiting the Source—she'd proved she was capable of killing. Who knew what could make her do it again?

Ashlyn thrashed, tangling herself in the shower curtain. Her wolf must be shredding her inside, trying to get out. He remembered the willfulness of his own wolf during puberty, when all he wanted to do was fight. To establish dominance. It was the natural order of things, each animal searching for rank among its kind. As an Alpha himself, Kepler could've broken away to form his own pack. But he'd reigned his wolf in, forced himself to behave. *Until tonight.*

How was he supposed to assure Ashlyn she could handle being a shifter when he couldn't even control his own beast?

Her icy-blue eyes flashed, and he caught a glimpse of her cream-colored wolf, fur darkened to a buff gold by the water. But then her human form solidified once more. Her teeth were bared with effort, knuckles white as she clutched the plastic curtain while the magic continued to swirl around her.

His chest swelled with pride. Her wolf was Alpha, but it seemed the human part of his mate was just as fierce. His wolf's urge to claim her grew stronger, and he took a step forward. *She will bear us strong pups.*

Years ago, Kepler had discovered that his wolf was naturally competitive. He used that weakness now. *Her control shames us, wolf. She does not wish to join you like this.* His wolf stopped moving and considered that. *We must prove our worth to her before she accepts us.* Kepler slowly, painfully, mastered his beast, concentrating on conforming his limbs to their human dimensions until he crouched naked in the growing puddle of water on the linoleum.

Ashlyn gaped at him with eyes round as full moons, her pink and blue hair plastered darkly against her scalp. Her shoulders began shaking. Was she crying? Laughing? He couldn't tell, but she was obviously hysterical.

He pulled a loose towel from the nearby hamper and wrapped it around his hips before easing toward her. The remains of his slacks lay in sodden scraps over the bathroom floor. Taking her face between his hands, he looked into her eyes. "You did well. You controlled her."

She panted and shuddered, her voice emerging as a squeak. "You're... you're one, too."

Kepler blinked in surprise. He'd assumed she'd known he was a shifter. Her wolf should've told her that right from the start. But she was new to the supernatural world. "Yes."

"I thought this only happened in movies with bad hair and fangs." Her voice shook.

He couldn't help the smile tugging at his mouth. *Sense of humor, even under stress.* She was strong. "I'd like to think we shifters are sexier than those in movies, but there is a kernel of truth in those myths." He reached up and turned off the water, then pulled a clean towel from the bar on the wall, wrapping it over her torso. "Your wolf is really strong, Ashlyn. Stronger than most. She's what we call an Alpha. You're going to have trouble controlling her."

Ashlyn pinned one arm over the towel and kicked free of the clingy shower curtain before struggling to her feet. "This can't be real. I bet I'm going to wake up in the morning with a monster hangover." She choked off another bubble of semi-hysterical laughter. "Where are my clothes?"

She thinks she's hallucinating. "It's real." He stood and turned off the water. "Your clothes are in pieces back in the alley."

Her eyebrows drew together, and she stared at the

scraps of his pants scattered across the bathroom. He could see the shallow rise and fall of her breathing as she clutched the towel around her naked body. Then she stood taller, seeming to find her resolve, and stepped past him toward the door. "I'm going home."

He threw out an arm to bar her way. She'd kept remarkable control of herself a few minutes ago, but that didn't mean she was good to go. There were a million triggers out there, from chihuahuas to other shifters. "You can't go until we figure out how this happened, and definitely not until I'm sure you have control of your animal."

The Alpha in her eyes flashed blue. "You can't tell me what to do. I must be drunk. I'm not in control of my faculties."

"You're not drunk, Ashlyn. This isn't a dream." He shoved her toward the mirror over the sink, pressing his chest against her back to hold her steady. She struggled as he jabbed a finger at the mirror. "Look at yourself. Really look."

She met his reflected gaze, then turned her attention to the bite on her shoulder. It had almost healed, and she ran her fingertips over the crescent of angry pink scar tissue, confusion filling her eyes.

"Shifters heal faster than humans," he said close to her ear. "Don't look at that. Look into your eyes."

She lifted her chin slowly. The glow of her Alpha flashed in her eyes, proof the animal was hovering close to the surface, eager to emerge at the slightest weakness. She stiffened, her skin heating under his hands. *She's going to shift.*

"No." Kepler spun her to face him. "Do not let her control you."

She trembled and bared her teeth. The glow in her eyes subsided. Gulping a breath, she shrugged his hands away. "I killed that man, didn't I?"

"He attacked *you.*" His hands clenched into fists at the thought of it. Born of violence and into violence, his mate would forever bear more than the scar on her shoulder from tonight, and he hated that. "That shifter was a rogue. An outlaw. Your wolf only acted in self-defense."

She swallowed. "What's going to happen now?"

He hesitated, realizing he didn't know. The Council should be informed. Ashlyn wasn't supposed to be a shifter. *They'll lock her away to study her. Or kill her outright.* He growled out loud, swallowing the sound when she shrank away.

Taking a step back to give her space, he inhaled through his nose, calming his wolf's instincts. Ashlyn had no pack, no family, no ties to anyone except him. *My mate.* Which she probably didn't even comprehend. Humans didn't experience pairing the same way shifters did. "I'm going to protect you."

A sarcastic chuckle shook her. "From what? Seems like my wolf has protecting me covered."

"I've been tracking rogue shifters for over two years now, and this is the first time something like this has happened. I don't understand how you're now a shifter."

"I got bit, remember?"

He shook his head. "Contrary to popular myth, a bite doesn't turn you into a shifter. You're either born as one or become one after drinking from the Source."

"Oh. Maybe someone slipped some of that stuff in my drink."

"Impossible. The magic only works inside the glacier cave. And the cave only opens when it chooses. I'm not even certain the cave can be found unless the aurora is out."

"So this isn't an infection. It's magic." She turned back toward the mirror and examined herself. "Can we break the curse?"

The pit of his stomach twisted. She'd called it a curse. She didn't want her wolf. *Of course she doesn't.* But if she went back to being human, what did that mean for him? Shifters were only granted one destined mate. Even so, he would never want her to live a life she didn't choose. He swallowed his selfishness and shrugged. "If this is a hex, then it may be possible. Do you know any witches?"

She gaped at him from her reflection. "Witches are real, too?"

He smiled grimly and nodded. "And vampires, dragons, mermaids, gargoyles—all the myths and legends are, in one way or another, true."

Her chest heaved with rapid breaths, gaze locked

with his for a few heartbeats. Then she stepped away from the sink, lifting a black tee shirt from the top of the hamper and pulling it over her head with one hand. The shirt fell almost to her knees over the towel which she let fall to the floor. "I need to go home."

Damn. All he wanted to do was peel that shirt back over her head and carry her to his bedroom. But now wasn't the time to play at being mates. Once they had this mystery unraveled, he'd talk to her about that. "You need to stay with me until we know what's going on. If your wolf breaks free, the local pack won't ask questions or give you a chance to explain. They'll exterminate you."

"The… pack? As in, wolf pack? Are there a lot of you?"

He forced a smile and spread his palms. "A few," he answered, thinking of the various packs scattered across the state. He hadn't registered with any of them, but he'd never been much of a joiner. His Alpha tendencies got in the way, and he didn't want to maintain a pack of his own. It would get in the way of his job. Plus, he liked being a lone wolf. "There's a lot you need to learn now that you're a shifter."

Her lips thinned, and she shook her head. "I really do need to go home. My cat needs to be fed."

"You have a cat?" It wasn't unheard of for shifters to own pets, but an Alpha wolf owning a cat was going to be interesting.

Her face paled. "Oh my God. Will my wolf try to hurt Mr. Mew?"

He put a hand on her shoulder. "Your wolf will probably be fine with it. It's the cat's reaction I'm worried about."

"I've had Mr. Mew since I was in high school."

"Let me get you a pair of sweats, then we'll both go. I'll make sure you don't do anything to hurt your cat."

CHAPTER FIVE

The witch sat ensconced in the corner near the DJ station, her spell of shadows making her all but invisible as the police cleared the bar. She didn't need to see the body in the alley to know who it was. The shifter's death was her fault, just like all the previous deaths. Why did she keep trusting that things would turn out different? Her previous coven leader had been right—she was in over her head and every time she tried something new, she seemed to sink even deeper. This entire project had gone spectacularly wrong from the moment she'd sent her familiar to investigate a reported hellmouth in Arizona.

Uncertain what to do next, she stared into a half-empty beer bottle someone had left behind. She could summon the agathion using any common glass vessel, and a part of her took satisfaction in seeing him inside the swill left behind by some drunk. Unlike their full-blooded djinn cousins who came to Earth to prey on hapless human souls, an agathion could not come all the way through to manifest a physical form and was generally considered harmless.

Except this one.

Right now, the tiny form of the man inside the bottle gripped her familiar in one hand, stroking the auburn fur between the ferret's eyes. Or should she say eye? The monster had plucked one of Hamilton's orbs from its socket the first time the witch had dared refuse one of his demands. Her familiar was trapped because of her, and she'd do whatever it took to free him.

She prayed the monster wouldn't punish Hamilton because of tonight's disaster. Her hex had barely lasted a few hours this time. Keeping her voice low, she gritted between her teeth, "You promised you'd keep this host alive."

"My dear, you worry too much." Violet sheet lightning feathered the agathion's skin. "This has been a most splendid evening. Far better than I expected."

Sickness at his cavalier attitude mixed with guilty relief that perhaps the agathion was finally satisfied. "Does that mean you'll let Hamilton go?"

He tilted his head. "Silly thing." His glowing eyes felt as if they might laser cut his way out of the bottle. "We're not finished. I need you to track down a newborn shifter."

Her blood turned to ice. Hexing adults was

distasteful enough, but an infant? Out of the question. "I draw the line at babies, you monster."

She made eye contact with Hamilton and swallowed past the lump in her throat. The mental thread she and her familiar usually shared had been disrupted by the agathion's magic, but she knew Hamilton would support her in this decision, even if it meant his death.

The agathion laughed, his voice crackling to match the storm on his face. "Not a child, a newly transformed shifter. The one I made in the alley. She will be my key."

The witch glared into the bottle. The agathion wanted to inhabit a human much the way a shifter's animal did, which would let him walk free like other djinn. She'd only balked a little when he revealed his desire. After all, there were already djinn walking the Earth. What was the harm in one more? But she was fine-tuning his hex on the lives of these shifters, and the death toll was mounting, as was her guilt.

"You said this shifter would be the one."

"I have finally discovered the missing element. This time the hex will be permanent."

Chewing her lip, she thought about refusing. The monster reached for Hamilton's other eye, and she shook the bottle. "Fine. But permanent or not, this is the last one. I do it, and you let Hamilton go."

The ferret wriggled between the agathion's slender fingers, and the monster pressed his face against her familiar's whiskered cheek. "But we've grown so fond of each other, haven't we Hamilton?"

Her familiar twitched the tip of his tail, the only form of support he dared offer, but she knew it for what it was. He was ready for this to end, too, one way or another.

"I mean it," she insisted. "After this, we're done."

The agathion's lips parted in a sharp-toothed smile. "If you succeed at this, I'll no longer need your services. Now, hurry and find her. The hellmouth is strongest while the aurora is active, and I don't know how much longer it will last."

She set the bottle on the table. "I need you to say it. I find this shifter, and you let Hamilton go."

"Find her and hex her, and I will release your pet."

Her mouth tasted like ashes. One way or another, this was going to end badly. Even so, she nodded. "Where do I start?"

CHAPTER SIX

*A*shlyn watched Kepler disappear through a doorway she assumed must be his bedroom. Emerging a few minutes later wearing jeans and a red tee shirt with a computer buffering icon and the words *I'm thinking*, he held out a neatly folded pair of gray sweats and clean tee shirt.

"Thank you." Her hand brushed his as she accepted the clothing, and she felt the urge to *bite* him, for Christ's sake. Her teeth ached for it. She breathed deeply and tried to clear her head, confused by the urges roiling inside her. If she wasn't thinking about biting Kepler, she was thinking about fucking him. The primal way he'd driven into her had been the most amazing sexual encounter she'd ever experienced. Did shifters feel sex in a different way?

Shoving her legs into the sweats, she cinched the drawstring tight around her waist and rolled the pant legs so she didn't step on them. When she exchanged the hamper tee shirt for the clean one, she felt a twinge of regret, but the clean one still smelled vaguely of Kepler, which she found calming.

"Ready," she said.

Kepler picked up a set of keys from a table in the hall and led her outside to his Jeep. They backed out of the driveway and, after she gave him her address, they maneuvered the dark streets in silence. She glared at her hands as if she could see through her skin to the wolf's paws beneath. *This can't be real.* But despite how normal her hands looked at the moment, she knew the beast inside her was there, waiting to break free.

At the curb outside her apartment building, Kepler climbed out of the Jeep and went around to open her door for her. A silly part of her wanted to tell him she'd had a lovely evening, as if they'd just come back from a date. Accepting his supportive hand, she slid from the seat, bare feet hitting the chilly dirt that was supposed to be a lawn but that never managed to grow more than weeds. The sweet scent of the crushed plants reminded her of chamomile.

She led him onto the cracked cement path bordered by huge spruce trees and followed it to the unsecured entry stairway. There, she paused and looked upward at her door. "Are you sure I won't hurt Mr. Mew?"

Tender concern softened Kepler's masculine features, and butterflies took wing in her stomach. He put a gentle arm around her shoulders. "I won't let you hurt your cat." His gray eyes didn't have the glow she'd seen when he shifted, but they still felt warm on her. The air between them filled with tension, like the weather before a thunderstorm. Inside her, the wolf rose toward the surface. *Bite him. Mark him.*

Trembling, she shrugged off his arm and climbed the stairs to her apartment. Only at the door did she realize she didn't have her purse or keys. Not even her phone with her landlord's number in it, not that she'd want Gerome to see her like this.

Kepler's presence felt warm behind her. "What's wrong?"

"I'm locked out."

"Ah." He moved to the door handle and examined it. "I've learned a thing or two being a criminal investigator. Let me try."

Within a minute, he had the door open. "You should really use your deadbolt."

She was hardly listening as the familiar scents from inside her apartment washed over her. The light sandalwood from her essential oil diffuser was strongest, but beneath that she could smell the overripe bananas on the counter and the acrid smell of Mr. Mew's litter box. Her geriatric cat was nowhere in sight, but he could usually be found curled up next to the radiator in her bedroom.

Thankfully, she felt no urge to hunt down her pet, at least not to kill him. Her head was a jumble of denial and rationalization, but the wolf inside her seemed content, at least for the moment.

"Mr. Mew?" she called, stepping inside and moving slowly toward her bedroom.

Kepler followed close behind, a calming presence as she flipped on the bedroom light. Mr. Mew wasn't in his usual spot, but her nose told her he was nearby.

"He's under the bed," Kepler said.

Heat crept up Ashlyn's face as she realized her purple vibrator lay among the rumpled white sheets. Had Kepler seen it? She cut him a glance from the corner of her eye, noting the whisper of a smirk on his face. Damn, of course he had. She flipped the blankets over the sex toy before bending to look under the bed.

A whiskered orange face looked back at her from near the headboard. "Mr. Mew? It's me. Come on out."

The cat growled and scrunched himself against the wall. Her stomach churned. He usually came right to her. "I think he knows I'm different."

"Maybe he'll come out if you feed him?" Kepler said. "I don't know much about cats."

It was worth a try. Ashlyn ushered Kepler out of the bedroom toward the kitchen and opened a can of cat food for Mr. Mew. The fishy scent made her mouth water. *Gross.* But she'd been hungry since before the party, and now her stomach felt like a black hole.

She plopped the food into the cat's dish and turned back to her almost empty cupboards. All she had on hand were five mojito cupcakes that hadn't fit in the box for the party. She peeled back the paper on one and took a huge bite, unconcerned about the frosting she could feel stuck to her lips. The sweet mint frosting and lime flavored cake tasting nothing like a real mojito, but she stuffed the rest of the cupcake into her mouth. "I'm so hungry," she said around the cake.

Kepler frowned. "I'm sorry, I should've offered you something to eat or drink at my house."

At the kitchen door, Mr. Mew appeared, pausing with one paw forward. She smiled at him and he gave her a reproachful look before edging along the far wall toward his dish. At least it was progress. She couldn't blame him for needing time to get used to her.

She went to the sink and filled her coffee maker while making a point of not looking at Mr. Mew. "Would you like some coffee?" She glanced sideways at Kepler, who was watching her cat. "I also have tea and cocoa."

"Coffee would be nice, thank you."

As the smell of coffee filled the kitchen, she grabbed the other cupcakes and moved to the small table in the corner near Mr. Mew's dish. Her cat kept a wary eye on her as he ate, but didn't run away. She blew out a shaky breath, relieved that things might be returning to normal. *Other than the fact you're now a supernatural being.* And there was a sexy wolf shifter standing in her kitchen.

Kepler was still watching her cat. Hopefully not

with hunger. After all, he was a wolf like her. Hoping to distract him, she held out a cupcake. "Want one?"

"Thanks." Kepler sat across from her and took it.

Ashlyn shucked a second treat from its paper and took a huge bite, unable to refrain from being impolite. She was so damn hungry, it was insane. Maybe being a wolf required a lot more calories. *Hmmm.* Eating as much as she wanted would be a nice perk if it was true.

Kepler carefully peeled back the paper and swept his strong tongue over the frosting.

She stopped chewing, hunger forgotten as she imagined that tongue—Kepler's tongue—licking her instead. Her nipples hardened against her tee shirt and heat pooled between her thighs. Even the way his fingertips held the cupcake was sexy and made her yearn for his touch. Fuck, she could smell her own arousal, which made her more horny. What was wrong with her?

She swallowed her bite, realizing she must look like an animal wolfing down food, then giggled, realizing how true that was.

Kepler tilted his head, his eyes deep pools she wanted to fall into. "What's so funny?"

"I'm wolfing." She cackled, feeling a little insane.

His eyebrows pinched, then he seemed to get it and chuckled before taking a huge bite of his own cupcake. "Mmmhmm."

Damn, he was sexy. She wanted to lick the frosting off his lips. And anywhere else he might like to put it…

She set her half-eaten cupcake down just as the coffee maker beeped. She was going to ignore it, but Kepler rose. She watched his gorgeous ass as he filled two mugs. Her hands itched to grab it, and it took all her willpower to resist.

He brought the mugs back to the table and set one in front of her before reclaiming his seat. She was about to tell him to forget the coffee when he said, "So. I'm sure you've thought of a ton of questions."

Her mood broke, all her worry rising to the surface. This pendulum of emotions and desires was wearing her out. Taking a breath, she said, "You said something about a witch. If this is a curse, can we break it?"

Quiet filled the room for a few moments as he seemed to think about his answer. "I honestly don't know," he said. "Tell me everything that happened leading up to you being attacked."

She told him about the bachelorette party and feeling sick. "I thought a bouncer had come to check on me. The next thing I knew, I had blood all over me and the guy was dead."

"You'd never met him before?"

"I don't think so. But a lot of people come into the bakery, so it's possible."

"He didn't say anything?"

"Oh, wait, he did. He said thank you." She recalled the look of gratitude in the man's eyes before the life faded from them. "He… thanked me for killing him?"

Kepler frowned and sighed. "When something,

usually a traumatic event, causes a shifter animal to go insane, we call them rogues. They become violent, rabid, sometimes suicidal."

"How awful." Ashlyn's throat ached.

He nodded. "Rogue shifters are rare. But about two years ago, there was an unexplained surge of cases. The only way to handle a rogue is to kill them before they hurt someone. My brother actually had to put one down that threatened his mate."

Something about the way he said "mate" flushed her entire body with heat. She sipped her coffee to cover her burning cheeks.

"Doctors eliminated the possibility of infection," he continued. "That left magic as the most likely cause, but we were never able to track down the witch responsible. And there were never any reported cases of an attack creating a new shifter."

"Never?" She tried to recall what he'd said about shifters earlier—they were either born or had to drink water from a glacier. "Are you sure someone couldn't have put some of that glacier water in my drink?"

"It's been tried, believe me." He shook his head. "The water becomes normal water if it's removed from the cave."

She swallowed, realizing he wasn't offering her any solutions. *I'm a freaking werewolf, now.* What did that mean for her? "If we can't undo this, if I'm no longer human, can I ever go back to my normal life?"

Kepler nodded. "There are plenty of shifters living

out in the open among humans—myself included. Nothing needs to change for you as long as you keep your wolf under control."

"How do I do that?" She gripped her mug with both hands, letting the hot ceramic grow uncomfortable against her palms. "Lock myself up during the full moon?"

He chuckled. "The full moon thing's a myth. Shifters can assume their animal form at any time."

"You mean I'm going to feel like this all the time?" She groaned and covered her eyes with one hand. "I was hoping it was like PMS or something."

This time he outright laughed. "Sorry, I shouldn't laugh. But your sense of humor is adorable." His phone buzzed, and he reached into his back pocket to retrieve it. He grimaced and tapped the screen. "I have to take this. Hey, captain."

Although Ashlyn could clearly hear the voice on the other end, she wasn't listening. *He thinks I'm adorable.* The wolf inside her felt all wiggly. *You like him, don't you?* she asked. The wolf grew even more wiggly, which made sense, she supposed. Kepler was the only other shifter she knew.

"I'll be in the office soon." Kepler hung up and shook his head, gaze full of apology. "If I don't get some reports filed, there will be all sorts of questions we don't want to answer. But I don't want to leave you alone."

She glanced toward Mr. Mew, who was now

cleaning a front paw with long strokes of his tongue. Apparently, a full belly had persuaded him that he didn't need to hide from her. "You can go. I think I'm okay."

Kepler took a deep breath and let it out slowly, his gaze locked on hers. Then he nodded and rose. "I can't believe how well you're handling… all this." The hint of a blush tinted his cheeks. "You're a remarkable woman, Ashlyn."

Heat flooded her face, and she smiled. God, she liked him.

He moved to her side of the table, placing a finger under her chin. "But don't leave the apartment, okay?" His voice was edged with concern. "There are lots of things that could trigger your wolf, and I'd feel better if I was around to help until you get used to her."

She gripped his wrist, liking the sound of him sticking around. "How long do you think you'll be gone?"

"A couple of hours, tops." His full palm now cradled her jawline. "I have to pop over to the Soldotna office to file paperwork. I'll be as quick as I can." He bent and brushed her mouth with his.

The feather light touch sent a fire through her that pooled between her legs. She had to force her fingers to let go of his wrist as he pulled away. She'd use the time he was gone to clean up her apartment. *Especially the bed*. Because when he came back, she had plans.

CHAPTER SEVEN

Kepler drove the dark, empty streets faster than he should've, but he didn't like leaving Ashlyn on her own. She'd handled her wolf well, at least after the first couple of changes, but that didn't mean she had complete control. *What will happen when she meets another shifter? Or a vampire?* One of the shifter packs in Fairbanks ran a tour company that specifically catered to the blood-sucking supernaturals and their love of long winter darkness, and he'd already noticed an influx even this far south.

"She'll be fine," he muttered out loud as he stomped on the gas, taking advantage of a straight stretch of road. The office was only forty minutes away, but might as well have been hours. Days, even. His wolf felt all bristly inside him, making it very clear he didn't want to be separated from his mate, especially when she was as yet unclaimed. *Claiming her might not even be an option.* His wolf didn't like that thought. But Ashlyn had been very clear about wanting to return to being human. There was a good chance she'd also reject having a mate.

He hadn't done a very good job explaining what it meant to be a shifter. She knew about the animal form and rapid healing, but he hadn't told her she'd gain mental telepathy if she joined a pack or that she could potentially live for hundreds of years. Was that even possible to become human again? A shifter's animal form was as much a part of them as their heart or brain and living without it was unheard of. But then, Ashlyn hadn't acquired her animal in the usual fashion. For all he knew, her condition was temporary.

This situation was bigger than he could handle alone, but he wasn't comfortable handing her over to the pack or Council as if she was just any shifter. He needed advice, preferably from someone who not only understood shifters but also magic. Digging out his phone, he voice-dialed his brother's house. Adrian answered after the second ring, "Hey, Kepler, how's the new job?"

"Fine, fine. I actually need to talk to Darcy. Is she around?" Kepler's sister-in-law was a witch, much to the distaste of his parents' pack. But after she stood up for Adrian at a wrongful death hearing, Kepler had welcomed her to the family with open arms. He'd never been one to look down on other supernaturals, anyway.

"She's making breakfast for the kiddo," Adrian said. "Let me get her."

After a minute, Darcy said, "Hi, K-kepler." Her stutter had gotten better since he'd first met her, but still came out when she was uncertain. "Is everything all right?"

"Do you know of any spells that can turn a human into a shifter? Or mimic a shifter's ability, even temporarily?"

"Hmm," she took a breath and spoke slowly. "If a witch has a familiar, she can mentally communicate with it and sometimes see through its eyes. Does that count?"

"No, I'm looking for something that actually changes someone into an animal."

"There are legends about skin walkers—witches who can change into animals—but that magic was banned centuries ago along with raising the dead or other types of necromancy."

"But it could be done. Could the witch target someone else with the spell? A human?"

"I'm not sure. I never studied it in detail. What's going on, Kepler?"

He sighed and slowed for an empty school bus that was trundling its way toward the sports center. "Last night a rogue attacked a human. Now she's a shifter."

"Oh my God. That's really bad. Dangerous c-creatures are attracted to skin walker magic, things that have not walked on Earth for millennia. Every time a skin walker shifts, it opens a hellmouth—not one like your Source, where the spirit animals regulate access or the ley lines where the witches keep watch, but a chaotic portal. Uncontrolled. It can give monsters a chance to slip through."

His throat tightened. "Monsters like what?"

"D-demons, for one. Dragons. Djinn."

He laughed uncomfortably, knowing that Ashlyn would probably make a joke about the three evil D's if she heard that list. But this was no laughing matter.

Darcy continued. "If this human is being targeted by a skin walker, every time she shifts, she attracts these creatures. You need to bring the local coven in on this investigation. They might be able to use the new shifter to trace the magic back to its creator. What's the name of the pack leader up there? I'd be happy to make introductions."

"I haven't told the pack." And now that he knew about this spell, he was even more reluctant. Their knee-jerk reaction would be to kill Ashlyn and eliminate any risk that the curse might spread.

"Kepler! Why not?"

"They'll kill her before her new ability can cause any damage or spread to others." His entire body flushed with rage at the thought.

"Oh." Darcy let out a shaky breath. "Well, considering what's at stake—"

"No!" A growl rose up the back of his throat. "You don't understand. She's my mate."

"Oh. Shit."

"Yeah, oh shit." He made a hard right into the empty parking lot in front of the Trooper offices. His captain's Bronco wasn't in its usual spot, so at least he could file his report without needing to make small talk with the human. "Thanks for the advice, Darcy. I need to go."

Cutting the connection before she could say anything else, he parked in front of the station and headed inside.

As he skulked past Regional Director Finch's doorway, a deep voice barked out, "Stone! Where the fuck have you been? Get your ass in here."

Kepler let out a slow breath. He'd hoped to slip by without being noticed, but should've known the grizzly shifter would be lying in wait. The guy treated his office like a den, and Kepler wondered if he ever left his desk.

Stepping inside, Kepler said, "I can explain, sir."

"Well, start talking." The brawny director tapped the surface of his desk with one thick finger. As usual, his dark brown hair looked like he'd been running his hands through it, and his eyes were bloodshot. "Officer Bennett reached out to me from the Kenai P.D. and told me this is a shifter case. Why am I hearing it from him before I hear it from you?"

Closing the door behind him, Kepler clenched his jaw. *Dammit, Cal.* Probably trying to rack up brownie points. "I was detained by another matter. I'll post an official statement that this was a bear mauling."

Finch grunted in discontent. "Why do people always have to blame a bear?"

Kepler shrugged apologetically. "Sorry, sir. This is Alaska and people always assume it was a bear."

"Hmph. And what other matter took precedence over the investigation?" Finch rested his elbows on his desk, fingers steepled. As the Regional Director and the only other shifter in the office, Finch acted as the liaison between law enforcement and shifter leadership.

"A personal issue. I have it under control now." Kepler put a hand on the door to go.

"Wait." The director's voice carried the weight of an Alpha command. Kepler's spine stiffened, and he turned back to Finch to find the man's dark eyes boring into him. "You're acting mighty strange. Anything you want to get off your chest?"

For a moment, Kepler considered telling the director everything, but his wolf wouldn't allow him to speak. Finally, he managed to say, "The dead man fits the description of the other rogues I've been chasing. We might have a new lead, that's all."

"So your absence has nothing to do with the naked woman you helped flee the scene?"

Shit. Cal must've seen her. Kepler pulled out the chair facing Finch's desk and reluctantly took a seat. It had been too much to hope that he could keep

Ashlyn a secret, but he still might be able to shield her from the pack. In an even voice, he described how he'd discovered Ashlyn hiding in the dumpster, the obvious victim of an attack. "Her wolf took down the rogue. She was traumatized, as anyone would be, and her animal was feeling protective. I felt that removing her from the scene would help calm her down."

Finch folded his hands on his desk and leaned forward. "So, where is she now?"

Of course Finch already knew she wasn't in pack custody, which was where Kepler should've taken her. "I took her to my house." He swallowed thickly, feeling strange about the next words on his tongue. "She's my mate, sir."

"Goddammit, Stone." Finch's eyes flashed with grizzly rage. "Anything else you want to tell me about this?"

There was only one thing that might excuse his lack of protocol, one thing another shifter would understand. "This was the first time I've met her, sir. I think the mating hormones muddled my thinking." The admission made him seem weak, but he'd do whatever it took to protect Ashlyn. "But I have it under control now."

A flicker of understanding crossed the grizzly shifter's features. "Ah, I see." He unclasped his hands and relaxed back into his desk chair. "What an unfortunate turn of events. You know I'm going to have to relieve you of duty on this investigation. The pack can take over from here."

Kepler's muscles tensed. The pack didn't know Ashlyn, or if they did, they knew her as the human owner of the bakery. How was he going to explain her sudden shifter ability? They were already riled about the rogues. They'd probably exterminate first, investigate later. "This isn't something you can hand over to untrained personnel, sir. I've been chasing this rogue outbreak for years."

Shuffling through some papers on his desk, Finch scribbled on one and thrust it at Kepler. "Believe it or not, Stone, I know what I'm doing. I've worked with the pack on rogue cases before."

"This isn't a normal rogue—"

"Enough." Finch held up a palm to stop Kepler's argument. "I'm relieving you of duty for the next few days. Take the time and get to know your mate. Oh, and report to your Alpha. I'm sure he'll have questions."

Gritting his teeth, Kepler resisted the urge to remind Finch that he hadn't joined the local pack. And he had no intention on stopping his investigation or handing Ashlyn over for questioning. No matter what Director Finch ordered.

CHAPTER EIGHT

With Kepler gone, Ashlyn finished off the cupcakes and went to her bedroom to tidy up. Mr. Mew was hiding, and a pang of loneliness rolled through her. Would her cat ever like her again? The bedside clock said it was just after five in the morning. Normally, she'd be at the bakery already, pulling the first batch of scones from the oven. Luckily, today was Monday, the one day a week they were closed. If she didn't get things resolved by tomorrow, she'd have to call her cousin and let her know they'd be closed an extra day. Not that Lana would care, since she'd be out on her fishing boat, anyway, but she was technically still a partial owner until Ashlyn paid her off.

Ashlyn pulled Kepler's tee shirt up to her nose and breathed deeply. His scent lingered in the fabric, and her wolf found it calming. Was it possible to miss someone you'd just met? She couldn't stop thinking about the way he'd touched her in the shower, so gentle, then so passionate. She hoped he wouldn't take all day to return.

He has responsibilities, Ashlyn, she reminded herself. A job, friends, maybe even a girlfriend…

A growl slipped up her throat, and she swallowed it down. That thought hadn't occurred to her, but a man as sexy as Kepler had to have women throwing themselves at him all the time. The fast-forming intimacy between them felt special to her, unique, but that didn't mean he felt the same way. The rational part of her brain told her he wouldn't have gone to so much trouble for her if he didn't feel the same way. That he'd come back the moment he could. But the wolf inside her was demanding she go out and find him.

And her wolf was strong.

She'd found herself at the door twice before she even realized what she was doing, and now looked down to find she'd donned her coat. *No, wolf, we need to stay inside.* She peeled off her coat and purposefully put it back in the closet. Kepler had said her wolf was an Alpha and that she'd have trouble controlling it. She rolled her shoulders, trying to shrug off the prickly sensation she'd come to associate with the urge to shift. If only she could hear Kepler's voice—but she'd left her phone at the bar with her purse. Not that they'd exchanged numbers. Her wolf paced restlessly inside her. *What if he doesn't come back?*

"Stop acting like a foolish teenager, Ashlyn," she told herself and stomped to the kitchen. Perhaps more food would calm her and her restless wolf. She was staring into the refrigerator thinking about Kepler when the doorbell rang.

Her heart nearly leapt out of her chest. *It's him!* She hurried toward the door.

The bell rang again, and a female voice called, "Ashlyn? Are you in there?"

Muffy? Ashlyn's excitement plummeted into dread. She crept forward and peeked into the peephole. The bride-to-be still wore her party garb, although the tiara was missing, and she held Ashlyn's purse in one hand.

Kepler'd said not to go anywhere, presumably so she wouldn't hurt someone again. Panic sent icy tendrils through Ashlyn's veins, and she shoved down the memory from the alley. *Pretend not to be home.* But she needed her phone and keys.

Outside, Muffy dug into the purse and retrieved Ashlyn's keys. She extended them toward the lock.

Oh, shit, she's coming in! Ashlyn scrambled for the door handle, uncertain if she meant to let her friend in or try to keep her out. But it was too late. The lock clicked, and the door swung open.

"Hello? Ashlyn?"

The door stubbed painfully against Ashlyn's bare toes. She backed out of the way on instinct. No hiding the fact she was home now. She couldn't even go hide under the bed with Mr. Mew.

Muffy's blue eyes filled with relief, and she flung her arms around Ashlyn's neck. "You're okay!"

Ashlyn tentatively patted Muffy's back in return. No urge to rip out her friend's throat, thank God, but she wrinkled her nose at the strange, almost ozone-like scent of Muffy's perfume. She'd never noticed that before. Her wolf was extra sensitive, it seemed.

"Yeah, I'm fine." She pulled away, clearing the raspiness from her throat. "Sorry for ditching like that."

"You went into the alley and never came back." Muffy held out Ashlyn's purse and keys. "They said someone was murdered out there. Did you see what happened?"

Nausea rolled through Ashlyn as she accepted her things. How was she supposed to answer? "I… I talked to a policeman," she started, liking that she was technically speaking truth. "He said not to discuss it with anyone."

Muffy glanced over her shoulder before stepping inside and closing the door. She narrowed her eyes and whispered, "You saw it, didn't you?"

Ashlyn swallowed and crossed her arms over her chest. Why did the air suddenly feel so stuffy? "I can't—"

"It's okay." Muffy took another step forward, bringing the ozone smell with her. "I know it wasn't a bear. It wasn't a natural animal at all. You're not going crazy."

Relief made Ashlyn feel weak in the knees. Even her

wolf felt it, giving her a soft whine of curiosity. There was only one way Muffy could know. "Are you a shifter, too?"

"Hell, no." Muffy cringed, nose wrinkling as if she'd caught a whiff of garbage. Then her eyes widened, and she made a strange gesture with her fingertips. "Wait, you're a shifter?"

Now Ashlyn was really confused. How did Muffy know about shifters if she wasn't one, too? "I really shouldn't talk about this."

Muffy frowned. "But I vetted you before the party."

"Vetted me? For what?"

"Witchcraft."

Ashlyn could barely take a full breath. Kepler'd said he thought there might be a witch involved in this. Was Muffy a witch? More importantly, was she responsible for what had happened? Ashlyn's wolf was remarkably quiet, but alert, as if poised to pounce if Ashlyn called on her. "Are you saying you're a witch? As in, cauldron-stirring, hocus pocus, abracadabra witch?"

Muffy laughed. "I don't know a single witch who says hocus pocus. Or abracadabra, for that matter. Yes, I'm a witch. When I met you at the bakery, I saw a spark of magic in your aura. We were going to ask if you wanted to join our coven."

Ashlyn's mouth fell open. Things were getting even more strange. "You thought *I* was a witch?"

"No, just someone with potential. Some humans don't realize it when they have the gift. We were going to offer to train you. But now this…" Muffy waived a hand to indicate Ashlyn's body.

"Do you know what happened to me?"

Muffy frowned and her gaze slid past Ashlyn to scan the apartment. "Your mate didn't explain things?"

Ashlyn frowned. "My mate?"

"The man who changed you."

The pain of the stranger's bite, his clawed grip on her shoulders, blood filling her own mouth... Ashlyn blinked against the memories. The inside of her mouth seemed too full of teeth, and her skin prickled with the need to shift.

Muffy's eyes narrowed. "You poor thing. You have no idea, do you?"

Ashlyn shook her head, every muscle in her body at war. She spoke between clenched teeth. "That man in the alley bit me, and now I seem to have become a werewolf."

Frowning, Muffy tilted her head. "Did you change right there in the alley, immediately after being bitten?"

Ashlyn nodded.

"That can't be right." Muffy took a step back, and Ashlyn's wolf detected a whiff of fear. "Shifters aren't supposed to have the ability to make new ones so easily. If they did, the entire planet would be overrun by the beasts."

Kepler'd said basically the same thing. Which meant this had to be a spell, like he thought. But she didn't think Muffy'd had anything to do with it. Even

Ashlyn's wolf agreed. She took a breath, uncertain how Muffy might take her next question. "Is it possible a witch did this to me? A hex or curse or whatever?"

"That's what I'm afraid of. I need to take you to the coven right away." Muffy opened the door and stepped outside. "Come on."

A sliver of hope took hold in Ashlyn's chest. "Can you make me normal again?"

"Newly turned vampires can be cured within a short time frame, but I don't know about shifters—or whatever it is you've become." Muffy sighed. "We need to take this to my coven leader. The sooner, the better, before the magic becomes permanent."

Ashlyn stared down at the purse she was clutching. Shifters. Witches. Vampires. She wasn't sure how much more she could take. All she wanted to do was go back to her busy days at the bakery and evenings snuggled up with Mr. Mew and a good book. *What about Kepler?* She couldn't let her unexplained feelings for him cloud her judgement. She'd just met him. If they were a good match, he'd like her whether she was a shifter or not. And if there was a cure, Muffy might be her only chance to get it.

"All right." Ashlyn's mouth twisted in a half-hearted smile. "Take me to your leader."

Kepler forced himself to obey the speed limit as he

joined the morning traffic on his route back to Ashlyn's apartment. He knew he couldn't handle this investigation alone, but who could he trust? *Cal.* He wasn't part of the pack, and although Kepler wanted to be angry with him, he knew Cal didn't deserve it. The police officer had only been following protocol when he'd sent his report to Finch. Besides, Cal would be able to keep Kepler abreast of the investigation now that Finch had booted him off the case.

He dialed Cal's number, about to hang up when a sleepy voice answered, "Fuck, Stone, what is it? I'm off duty."

"Sorry, but I need your help."

"I handed my report over to the MCU already."

"I know. I just spoke to Finch." Kepler took a steadying breath and explained the situation, including what his sister-in-law had told him about skin walker witchcraft.

"So is she a shifter or not?"

Kepler scowled. That was a decent question. "Fuck if I know."

A long pause filled the air before Cal asked, "Are you sure she's your mate?"

Kepler took a deep breath, trying not to be angry with his friend. "My wolf's not lying." Maybe it'd been a mistake to bring Cal into this. The other shifter wasn't part of the pack, but he did have a duty to protect the shifter community. He might decide to take the skin walker theory to the pack, which would only send them on a witch-hunt—literally. Kepler said, "Listen, if you're not willing to help, that's okay, just keep quiet until I get things worked out. You know how the local pack is. If they believe she's a danger, they'll exterminate her and ask questions later."

"Have you claimed her already?"

"Whether I've claimed her or not doesn't matter. She needs to be protected until we can investigate," Kepler ground out.

"Calm down, man. I'm asking valid questions. Are you certain she's not in on it with the witches or anything?"

That was something he hadn't considered, but the suggestion made him angry. "Jesus, Cal, she was shocked and terrified, not deceitful. Besides, I didn't smell witchcraft."

"Sorry, but I had to ask. We don't know enough about these rogues to rule anything out. For all we know, she's the vector spreading the outbreak. She could be making shifters think she's their mate."

Kepler's blood turned to ice. No, that couldn't be right. What he felt for Ashlyn was real. Gripping the steering wheel hard enough to make his knuckles turn white, he said, "My wolf would know the difference."

Obviously sensing he needed to tread lightly, Cal said softly, "Maybe I should meet her, too. See what my wolf thinks."

Much as Kepler hated to admit it, Cal made a good point. If the other shifter met Ashlyn and felt the same draw Kepler did, then perhaps the mate bond wasn't real after all. The thought of introducing another male to Ashlyn made Kepler's hackles rise, but he gave Cal her address. "Call me when you get here."

"Roger that." Cal hung up.

Kepler pulled up to the curb outside Ashlyn's apartment, jumped out of the Jeep, and loped toward the building, every inch of him burning to see Ashlyn again. To lay claim on her before Cal arrived. *That might be exactly what the witch wants*, he reminded himself. Outside her door, another scent permeated the hallway, one every shifter knew well. Ozone. A witch had been here. Skin crawling, he knocked.

No one answered. *Shit*. He tried the handle, but the door was locked. Glancing around for onlookers, he used his shoulder to force the door open with a loud crack.

Inside, everything looked and smelled the same. No sign of a struggle. He checked the kitchen, noting the empty cupcake wrappers in the garbage, then strode to the bedroom. The bed was now made, and Ashlyn's cat stared at him from where it was curled up on her pillow. Wherever she'd gone, it seemed to have been willingly.

He followed Ashlyn and the witch's scents outside to the street where the trail faded. They must've gotten in a car. To continue tracking, he'd need his wolf's senses, but he risked being seen if he shifted here.

Heart thudding against his ribs, Kepler glanced up and down the street.

Headlights approached, and Cal pulled up in his police cruiser. "What's wrong?"

"She's gone. And a witch was here."

Cal's nostrils flared. "Shit."

"Fuck it," Kepler muttered and shimmied out of his shoes and clothes. He was going after her, and he didn't care who saw him.

"I'm with you," Cal said, unsnapping his uniform shirt.

Within moments, Kepler's wolf let out a satisfied howl, breaking the silence of the morning, and started running.

Ashlyn clutched her dead phone in her lap, wishing she'd thought to leave a note for Kepler. Or anyone, for that matter. Her cousin only checked on her every few days at the bakery. Muffy didn't have a car charger, but offered to let Ashlyn use her phone. Unfortunately, Ashlyn hadn't memorized her cousin's number.

Muffy pulled onto a narrow dirt road plastered with bright yellow leaves. Pale mist muted the red and orange underbrush beneath the gray skeletal tree trunks. "Where are we going, anyway?" Ashlyn asked.

"Our coven leader, Tessa, runs a school out here. The solitude means there's less chance of mortals stumbling onto spell practice." Muffy patted Ashlyn's hand, palm cool against Ashlyn's skin. "She's a nature witch, a really good one. I'm sure she'll know how to help."

After following the road for what seemed like forever, they reached a tall, wrought-iron fence. Muffy entered an access code that made the gate roll aside. It automatically slid closed behind them as they pulled up to a large gray house with white trim. A series of raised garden beds held a few late-season flowers, and the grass paths between them were perfectly mowed and clear of the leaves that carpeted the lane and driveway. Fancy beveled glass panels on the front door glowed with warm yellow light from inside the house. Yesterday, Ashlyn would've thought the place was charming. Today, all she could think about was the witch in *Hansel and Gretel*.

Muffy cut the engine and got out, closing the car door with a solid thud. She hurried up the wide wooden steps toward the front door.

Ashlyn took a few calming breaths. Her wolf was curious rather than hostile, at least for now. Kepler'd warned her it would be hard to control, and meeting another person—another witch—made her nervous.

But she needed answers.

She opened the car door, letting the cool autumn air wash over her.

An older woman in jeans had opened the front door, her long silver hair in a braid over one shoulder. Wearing Xtra-Tuff boots, she reminded Ashlyn of her cousin if Lana was thirty years older. *Only a lot less friendly*. The woman scowled at Muffy and cut a look toward the car as Ashlyn climbed out. Ashlyn caught the tail end of her sentence as she approached. "...here was unwise."

Muffy looked over her shoulder at Ashlyn and signaled her to hurry and join them. "I couldn't leave her there alone. If the shifters discover her, they'll probably kill her on sight."

Ashlyn came to a stiff halt halfway up the steps. Kepler had mentioned a pack, but she'd thought they would only hurt her if she couldn't control her wolf. She stared at the witches a few steps above her, relieved she felt no urge to harm them. "Kill me? Why?"

The older woman studied Ashlyn. "Shifters are little more than animals." Her upper lip curled with what Ashlyn could only consider disdain. "They destroy what they don't understand."

Kepler's handsome face flashed in Ashlyn's mind. He hadn't tried to kill or even hurt her. He said he wanted to protect her. *He's special, though.* Her wolf agreed. When Kepler told her not to leave the house, she'd assumed it was so she didn't hurt anyone else. But what if it was to protect *her* from other shifters?

"Ashlyn, this is Tessa, our coven leader." Muffy grabbed Ashlyn's arm, pulling her the rest of the way up the steps. "Tessa, we have to help her."

Tessa sighed and pulled the door closed behind her. "Fine, let's have a look." She moved past Ashlyn down the stairs. "Bring her to my conservatory."

Muffy nudged her to follow, keeping close behind

Ashlyn as they walked the grass path between the garden beds, wisps of mist swirling in their wake. In the backyard, a small greenhouse with crenelated iron ridges and gables sat among late-flowering yellow shrubs. The glass walls were fogged over, masking the interior from view, but the moment Tessa pushed a sliding door aside to let them inside, the smell of warm soil and fresh sap hit Ashlyn. Three rows of potting tables took up the entryway, but then the space opened into what looked like a fairytale.

A huge, smooth-barked tree grew in the center of a circle of stones, and the ground beneath was a carpet of golden, lavender, and blue wildflowers. Tessa crunched over the gravel between the tables and stepped into the circle.

"How does this all fit into the greenhouse?" Ashlyn asked.

Muffy answered, "It's a sanctuary of sorts, a safe place to access strong magical energies. I can't really explain to someone who hasn't studied magic." She nodded in encouragement and nudged Ashlyn forward. "Go on."

Hesitantly, Ashlyn stepped over the stones and onto the wildflower meadow. A breeze caressed her cheek and running water trickled somewhere in the distance. The greenhouse walls faded from view, leaving her surrounded by nothing but meadow as far as she could see. Ashlyn glanced over her shoulder to where she'd left Muffy, but it seemed as if everything on the other side of the circle of stones no longer existed. "Can Muffy still see us?" she asked.

"Yes." Tessa bent and dipped her fingers into a tiny pool of water set among the gnarled roots of the tree. She flicked droplets into the air where they hovered like diamonds. Ashlyn gaped, unsure she was seeing right as Tessa repeated the motion until a sheet of droplets hovered in the air between them.

Amazed, Ashlyn asked, "What are you doing?"

"Casting a scrying spell. I need a closer look at your aura before we try to cure you. Take a deep breath," Tessa commanded. "This won't hurt, but you might find it a little disconcerting."

Muffy'd mentioned looking at her aura when she came into the bakery. Ashlyn inhaled deeply, stiffening as the sheet enveloped her. Although she could still see the meadow clearly, the thin film of water made her feel as if she'd just plunged into a cold ocean current. Her heartbeat pounded in her ears, and pressure buffeted her from all sides, throwing off her equilibrium. In her head, her wolf flailed as if trying to reach the surface.

Tessa green eyes deepened to almost black and her mouth moved, but Ashlyn couldn't hear what she said, only strange pinging and warbling that reminded her of flexing sheets of metal.

A howl rose above the metallic noise, her wolf no longer curious, but terrified.

Ashlyn couldn't exhale. Couldn't inhale. Couldn't move. Between herself and the witch, what felt like a chasm opened into another reality. A landscape of colors and shapes beyond anything that existed on earth. The scent of ash drifted from the breach, and a coldness reached for her, sharp as glass. Her mouth gaped to echo her wolf's cry.

Then the water that bound her evaporated. She collapsed to the ground, every muscle shaking as she tried to process what happened. Directly beneath her paws, the carpet of wildflowers had been rendered to blackened ash. Above her head, she heard voices, but they made little sense. *Unstable. Shifter. Hellmouth.*

Every instinct Ashlyn's wolf possessed knew that chasm had held death. Worse than death. Damnation. She had to get away. The pinging and warbling she'd heard lingered at the back of her mind, no longer the sounds of sheet metal, but more like an approaching storm. She couldn't get it out of her head.

Then somewhere in the distance, a wolf howled. The sound struck a chord deep in her chest. Steadied her. Brought her paws back to Earth. *Kepler.*

Lifting her muzzle, she let loose a cry that made the tree's leaves shiver overhead. Her wolf was in control. Her wolf would protect her. Her wolf would take her back to Kepler.

She lunged from the circle, the foggy greenhouse walls re-materializing around her. Without slowing, she crashed through the greenhouse siding. Glass penetrated her thick fur, cut fiery lines into her flanks, but she kept going.

Kepler, I'm coming.

CHAPTER TEN

Kepler and Cal stuck to the trees when possible, the afternoon fog helping them stay out of sight of traffic until the trail left the highway. Panting, Kepler turned onto a narrow, leaf covered lane. Ashlyn's scent had almost disappeared as the overpowering ozone smell of witchcraft grew stronger. There was more than one witch involved.

This is coven territory, Cal's voice flooded his head.

Kepler almost stumbled. Only mates or pack members could communicate while shifted. Kepler sent back, *You talking to me?*

Been listening to you count witches for the last ten minutes.

Kepler had experienced whispers of his Alpha power like this before, an inkling of what leading a pack might be like. He'd always pulled away and shielded himself, wanting to avoid any such ties so he could focus on his career. Now he was grateful for backup. *We may have a fight on our hands.*

Bring 'em on, Cal growled, never breaking his stride. His russet coat blended well with the dark autumn foliage, unlike Kepler's own pale gray. *Fucking witches.*

Ahead, a tall wrought-iron fence loomed from the mist surrounding the damp gray tree trunks, forming a palisade of spears. The carpet of leaves under Kepler's paws cushioned his footsteps as he approached the gate. Magic radiated off the barrier, a ward he was certain would be painful or maybe even kill him if he tried to leap over.

He sat on his haunches and growled.

What do we do now? Cal asked.

My mate's in there. Kepler shifted to his human form and took a step toward the entrance. "Guess I'm going to knock."

You're naked, man, Cal said, remaining in wolf form as he moved to block Kepler's path. *They aren't going to let you in.*

Kepler couldn't care less that he was naked. All that mattered was getting to Ashlyn, or at least stopping whatever the witches were planning to do to her. For the first time, Kepler regretted not being part of a pack. Not having immediate access to backup. "Go for help. I'll try to stall whatever the witches have planned for Ashlyn until you get back."

Without waiting to see if Cal complied, Kepler approached a keypad near the gate. Beyond the fence, running footsteps caught his attention as a big, amber-ruffed wolf appeared from the mist. *Ashlyn!* She was safe and alive. The wolf raced toward the gate with determination in her gaze. Kepler guessed her intent a moment before her body coiled to spring, his stomach flipping in alarm. "Ashlyn, no! It's warded!"

She cleared the fence in a graceful leap, but at the apex, her body convulsed in a shower of sparks. Her fur dissolved, and her limbs lengthened. She hit the ground in human form, sliding to a stop on her side against the wet leaves.

Kepler rushed over. "Ashlyn!"

She lay in a fetal position with her eyes closed, sides heaving and pink and blue hair tangled with leaves and twigs. Long scratches along her ribs seeped blood. He reached for her, furious the witches had hurt her. Her eyes flashed, and she bared her teeth, struggling to sit upright.

It took him half a second to realize her gaze wasn't on him. It was on Cal.

He spun to find the russet wolf with his paws braced wide, lips pulled back from his canines in a ferocious growl. The dark guard hairs on his ruff stood on end.

Kepler held both palms up. "Cal, it's okay. This is Ashlyn."

No words of response entered Kepler's head, only a snarl and a snap of teeth.

At least this answered the question about whether

Kepler's mating instinct was unique to him or not—Cal obviously felt no attraction to Ashlyn at all. Holding one palm up at the wolf, Kepler moved forward, infusing his voice with Alpha power. "Stand down, Cal."

Cal's yellow eyes flashed. Then, in a flurry of copper sparks, he shifted back to human form. He thrust a finger toward Ashlyn. "She's not a shifter."

"What're you talking about? You just saw her wolf, Cal."

"Can't you smell it?" Cal whispered roughly. "She's wrong, Kepler. All wrong."

Kepler turned back to Ashlyn. She sat with her back against a tree, both arms wrapped around her knees. The ozone scent was strong on her, as well as her amazing natural wildflower honey scent, but laced beneath was something more primal and raw. Blood. Wet leaves. An odor like burning coal. What spell smelled like that? He didn't know enough about witches to guess. "That's just the witches you're smelling, Cal. It will fade."

Somewhere on the other side of the fence, a car engine rumbled to life. A woman's voice floated through the fog, "Call everyone. We have to find her."

"Let's get out of here," Kepler whispered, taking Ashlyn by the elbow. "Can you walk?"

Although the cuts on her side had already begun to heal, Ashlyn blinked at him as if he spoke a foreign language.

Letting out a worried breath, he lifted her. She looped her arms around his neck as he carried her into the woods.

Cal followed sullenly behind, pushing through the undergrowth. After they'd put some distance between them and the fence, Cal asked, "Isn't that the woman from the bakery?"

"Yes."

"She's… something's not right. Not normal. We need to tell the pack. Hell, we need to bring the whole Council in on this one."

Kepler grit his teeth. "Not until I know they won't hurt her."

"What if she hurts you?"

Kepler rounded on him. "Does she look capable of hurting anyone right now?"

Cal stopped, concern darkening his freckled face. "You're under her spell."

"She's not a witch."

"She's also not a shifter."

"Fuck you, Cal. She's my mate."

"You haven't claimed her."

Kepler's teeth lengthened, pressing against his lips until his words slurred. "I'll claim her right here and now if that's what you need to prove she deserves protection."

"I'm not saying we shouldn't protect her. I'm saying we can't do it alone." Cal took a step back, his eyes flashing copper. "I'm going to tell the pack." In an explosion of sparks, he shifted and disappeared into the fog before Kepler could say another word.

Exhaling a long white plume of air, Kepler continued hurrying the opposite direction. A part of him knew Cal was right. They needed help. The strange smell on Ashlyn wasn't fading, and he knew in his heart what that meant. *She's been cursed.* But with what?

Ashlyn's arms tightened around his neck. "What's claiming?"

Kepler stopped walking, realizing he and Cal had been speaking about her as if she wasn't there. "This wasn't how I wanted to have this conversation."

"You said I'm your mate." Her voice had a sexy rasp to it that made his balls ache.

Looking into her eyes, he was glad to see the glazed look had gone away. She was so beautiful, amber cheeks flushed and lips slightly pursed. They were far enough from the witches' compound to take a breather, so he set her gently on her feet, keeping a hand at her waist to make sure she stayed upright before speaking.

"Every shifter has a perfect mate somewhere in the world," he said. "When we meet him or her, our wolf knows. It's fate. We can choose to accept the bond or reject it, but our wolves will always desire each other."

She stood motionless for several heartbeats, the forest's silence like a held breath. Finally, she asked, "Is that what I'm feeling?"

Relief flooded through him. *She feels it, too.* He

wanted to pull her close and kiss her, to run his hands through her hair and breathe in her honey scent. "Yes. We're mates."

Her eyes flashed blue, and he knew her wolf was giving approval. Hex or not, her wolf was real. Their connection was real. He lowered his lips to hers. She responded by putting both hands around his neck and kissing him back.

After a lingering moment, she broke the kiss to look at him again. "The witches were going to try to remove the curse, but I don't want to anymore. Especially if it would send my wolf to that place."

He frowned and pulled her hands from his neck so he could step back and look at her, still holding her wrists. "What place?"

"The coven leader was investigating my aura. But the spell she cast..." Ashlyn shuddered and hugged her arms around herself. "I swear, she opened a portal to hell, all roiling color and chaos. They even called it a hellmouth. My wolf didn't like the magic. *I* didn't like the magic. I shifted, and we ran."

"A hellmouth." The pit of his stomach felt like he'd just taken a bullet. His sister-in-law had used that word over the phone.

He dragged in a breath, sensing Ashlyn's wolf along with the slightly off scent he and Cal had argued about. *It must be the lingering scent of the hellmouth.* The Source was in essence a hellmouth, too, a portal that allowed shifter animals to find their hosts. He'd never been there, but her description resembled the stories he'd heard.

Taking her hand, he continued walking between the trees. "Remember I told you about the glacier, the Source for shifter magic?"

She nodded.

"Normally, a shifter who finds a human mate takes the human there to discover the new shifter's animal. But when we first met, I was too clueless to recognize you as my mate." He ran a hand through his hair, thinking about his first visit to her bakery. The shop had been busy, and the scent of baked goods so pervasive, he'd obviously missed her. But her wolf had recognized him. "I think your wolf was impatient. And we know she's a strong Alpha. I'm guessing she found another way to you."

Ashlyn pulled her hand free from his. "But the rogue… are you saying my wolf caused that shifter to get sick?"

Pausing at the lip of a shallow ravine, he shook his head. "The shifter outbreak started before we met. Your wolf just took advantage of an opening." He jumped down and held out a hand to Ashlyn. She took it and leaped down beside him. As they followed the gully, he described what Darcy had told him. "The magic is forbidden by the covens because it opens a hellmouth, a portal that can allow demons and other monsters through. In your case, it let your wolf through."

She halted and covered her mouth, eyes going wide. "Cal said I'm not a real shifter. Does that mean my wolf is a demon?"

Kepler cupped her face between both palms and looked into her eyes. "You're my mate and your wolf is real, no matter how you got her."

"But am I a real shifter?"

"You're going to discover that not all supernaturals get along. Shifters, witches, vampires—they all look down on each other. It's like racism among humans. To me, it doesn't matter. You're my mate and that's all that's important." He kissed her lightly and once more took her hand to keep walking.

She was silent for a short while before she said, "Would going to the Source make me a real shifter?"

"If you already have a shifter form, drinking from the Source will swap your animal out. You'd lose your wolf and end up with a moose or something." He shook his head, thinking about recent rumors about exactly that happening to a shifter up north.

Ashlyn giggled, then quickly sobered again. "Don't make me laugh. This is serious. The witches said I was unstable."

Unstable. How many times had he been called that in his youth? His mom used to joke about how he and his brother Adrian would never find a mate to calm them down. His heart thudded against his ribcage as he realized there was another way to stabilize a shifter's animal. The mating claim. Many shifters discovered a calmer version of themselves after claiming a mate. What if that was all Ashlyn needed?

He stopped next to a fallen tree and faced her. As they'd been walking, the mist had cleared, and a flock of wild geese flew in a V overhead, their honking barely audible in the brilliant blue sky. Sunlight made the golden leaves carpeting the ground look like something out of a painting. He pushed an errant strand of pink hair behind her ear. "We could try completing the mate bond. It might stabilize your wolf."

She stepped closer and ran both palms up his chest to once more circle his neck. "If claiming involves what I think it does, then what are we waiting for?"

He restrained himself, taking one more deep look into her eyes. "I want to make sure you understand. A claim means we're bonded for life. We'll be able to hear each other's thoughts, feel each other's emotions. As a shifter, you're going to live longer—hundreds of years, maybe. With me. You'll never be able to be with anyone but me."

She leaned into him. "And you with me?"

He nodded, the desire to taste her lips making it difficult to breathe.

She lifted her chin, bringing her mouth close enough he could feel her whispered words on his skin. "Then I'm yours."

CHAPTER ELEVEN

The witch sat in her rental car and gripped the steering wheel with both hands, refusing to look at the empty bottle strapped in the passenger seat. Well, not empty, exactly. Below the edge of her sunglasses, she could see a hint of swirling lavender light within the brown glass.

"I can fix this," she said out loud, uncertain how she was going to make that happen as she stared at the big gray house ahead.

She wasn't part of this coven, hadn't had to answer the summons. In fact, she'd be in grave danger if anyone suspected her of being in league with the agathion. But the coven had somehow caught wind about the shifter she was after. She had to find out what they knew and reach the shifter first. Her familiar's life depended on it.

She parked next to a beat-up Subaru under the

boughs of an old spruce tree and threw a reusable grocery bag over the growler. She could no longer dismiss the agathion like she used to, which worried her. He was getting stronger, even though she had yet to secure him an appropriate host. She locked the bottle in the car and turned toward the house.

The sun had crossed the sky and brushed the tips of the barren trees, setting the yard aglow with orange light. The air whispered to her of witches who'd recently passed through here. Now that the coven knew someone was casting death spells, they were duty-bound to purge the world of forbidden magic.

"Would help if I had Hamilton to help me," she muttered under her breath, longing for her familiar.

At the base of the steps, the breeze whispered something new. Something foreign. *The agathion's shifter?* Could the coven have captured it already?

Veering between the flower beds, she skirted the house until she reached a greenhouse. No surprise, it radiated magic. One of the panes had been shattered, leaving shards of broken glass scattered across the grass. No shifter here, but something had definitely happened.

A glance over her shoulder assured her no one was watching from the house's windows before she moved toward the wreckage. She lifted her sunglasses, squinting at the ground. Several glass shards were discolored with blood. *The shifter's?* The only reason she needed to find the shifter was to get a physical sample for the hex—blood, hair, skin, anything would do. This blood was already on glass, the perfect conduit for the agathion's power. Maybe things were finally going her way.

Maybe this could all be over soon, and Hamilton would be free.

Carefully plucking several shards from the grass, she wrapped tissue around them and placed them in her purse. Now to find a safe place to cast—

"Jen, you made it!"

Her heart nearly leapt out of her body at the sound of her name. She turned to find Muffy striding toward her from the house, lines of distress creasing her brow. Her sister grabbed her hand, tugging her toward the back door. "Thanks for agreeing to help. Come inside. Tessa has a plan."

A twinge of guilt soured Jen's stomach. Her sweet, unsuspecting sister had invited her to Alaska, hoping she'd like the coven enough to join. But everything Jen touched seemed to go to shit. She had no intention of poisoning the coven her sister had grown to love.

But she couldn't let the coven suspect she was behind the hexing. She'd just have to play along until she could break free and cast her final hex. Softening her face into a smile, she followed Muffy inside.

CHAPTER TWELVE

Ashlyn let out a slow breath, staring into Kepler's eyes. The golden glow there spoke to her wolf. His nearness ignited her passion. He was huge, strong, and *naked*, skin warm in the autumn chill. Her thighs quivered in response. *Fated mates.* Could a modern day relationship be built on something out of a fairytale?

Kepler seemed to think so. She loved how easy it was to lose herself in him. To trust that everything was going to be okay. He pulled her tight against him and secured his mouth against hers, tongue demanding entrance as if they'd kissed a million times.

She pressed herself against him as they kissed. She knew almost nothing about his life outside of the time they'd spent together, yet the emotion she felt was real and strong and pure. Forever with Kepler would be nothing shy of heaven. She wanted him more than she'd wanted anything in her life. It had been a whirlwind, but she couldn't believe how incredible it felt to love him. *I love him.*

"Claim me," she said.

Kepler's arms tightened around her, and he growled deep and low. He rolled his hips, letting her feel the hard length of his erection pinned between them. One of his hands slid over her naked ass and into the space between her thighs, fingers dipping into her waiting wetness. She gasped, arching her back to open herself up for his exploration. He delved between her folds, slipping along her lower lips with teasing slowness.

More accustomed to her wolf now, Ashlyn reveled in their heightened senses. Her wolf made her bold, more sure of herself. Releasing one hand from her grip around his shoulders, she slid her palm between them to find his shaft. Thick, rock-hard heat met her hand, and she wrapped her fingers around it, stroking upward.

His touch on her backside drew away, but before she could protest, he lowered her into a hollow of dry leaves beneath the roots of a fallen tree. The earth smelled raw, primal, matching the feelings growing inside her. This was so right, this moment with Kepler. *All things will be made right.* She had no idea if that was her wolf's thought or her own, but didn't have time to dwell on it.

Kepler knelt between her legs and dragged her ankles up over his shoulders. Her stomach dipped as she realized his intention. His tongue parted her slit, meeting her core in an explosion of sensation that made her gasp. He circled her opening once, then sucked gently on her sensitive nub.

She bucked upward with a moan. Her entire being wanted this, wanted him. His tongue flicked against her, making her body surge with pleasure. He worked her clit while she threaded her hands into his hair, rocking against his mouth. The pressure inside her expanded, racing down her thighs, tingling in her nipples. Her legs trembled, and she gripped handfuls of his hair as she climbed toward climax.

He plunged his tongue into her opening, throwing her over the edge into ecstasy. She screamed his name as he kept thrusting his tongue, thumb against her clit, extending her orgasm until she could no longer breathe.

When her muscles could take no more, he eased, letting her sink into bonelessness against the cushion of leaves. Her racing heart and ragged breathing made the world spin, and she closed her eyes. "Kepler, that was…" she couldn't finish between gulps of air.

He planted small kisses against her inner thigh, moving upward over her belly to her breasts. "You are," he nipped one nipple, sending an aftershock rolling through her, "the most beautiful," he nipped the other nipple, "woman on the planet."

She curled her fingers into his hair again, shuddering as he continued teasing each nipple, intensifying her aftershocks. Her core ached, tired yet yearning to be filled.

Wrapping her legs around his hips, she said, "I want you inside me."

Kepler moved to her mouth, kissing her deeply. The head of his cock was ready, pulsing at her entrance. He pushed into her slowly, surely, his eyes never leaving hers. She never wanted this moment to end. She tightened her quivering muscles around him.

He groaned, "You're so tight. So hot."

She lifted her hips, seating him fully inside her, feeling the pressure of him deep in her belly. He let out a shuddering breath, each of them still for a long moment, lost in each other's eyes. Lost in each other's bodies. God, she loved the way he covered her, as if he owned her. He pulled back slowly, beginning a rhythm. Increasing his tempo, he gripped the back of her neck, fire in his eyes.

She clutched his back, rising to meet his thrusts as he drove into her. When he plunged his tongue into her mouth, her teeth felt too sharp, but he didn't seem to notice. She opened wide, tangling her tongue with his, tasting him as she'd never tasted any man before. *Mine*, her wolf growled. The urge to bite him, to taste him, was growing inside her in a way she found both unsettling and exciting.

He continued kissing her, a form of claiming all its own, until the first tightening of her inner walls made her dig her nails into his back in anticipation.

Then his teeth were against her shoulder. Both her orgasm and the fire of his claim shot through her as a single sensation. She howled in pleasure, shudders coursing through her body before she clamped her mouth onto his shoulder in return. As her teeth sank into his smooth, hard flesh, he growled, thrusting hard and filling her with pulsing heat.

Locked together, they slowly relaxed, him still on top of her as she went limp against the cushion of leaves.

Kepler feathered his lips against her jaw. "Mine."

She smiled. "Mine."

His warmth felt like a protective shield. Then she felt a caress in her mind that was so full of tenderness, she wanted to cry. Kepler's silent voice sounded exactly like his regular one. *Ashlyn, can you hear me?*

I can! She'd never imagined being this close to another person, and it felt amazing. *The claiming worked!*

His arms around her tightened. *It did.* Pure joy infused his words. *We are bound. How's your wolf?*

She looked inside. Her wolf was all relaxed and melty inside her. *I don't know if she's stable or not, but she's certainly content.* She ran her fingertips along his jawline and smiled at the warm glow in his eyes. *Do my eyes glow like yours?*

He nodded. *Yes, but yours are glacier blue.*

Can humans see it? Or only other shifters?

Humans can see it, but most of them think it's a trick of

the light. Even so, you should be careful using your wolf's senses in public.

She nodded, then asked out loud, "If we're both shifters, does it mean our kids will be puppies?"

He chuckled. "Don't worry. Shifter kids don't experience their first change until puberty."

She grinned back, loving that he appreciated her humor. "What do we do next?"

He kissed her gently, then rose. Shadows were taking over the forest as the sun began to set. "We should've picked a better place and time for this. There are witches after you, and Cal could return with the pack at any moment."

The cool air gave her goosebumps as she climbed to her feet, worry taking over where contentment had been. "Can we outrun them?"

He shook his head. "Not forever." The glow in his eyes brightened as he looked at her. "I was hesitant to introduce you to the pack, but I think it's safe, now. As my mate, you're protected. They can no longer kill you as an outsider. I just need to introduce you and we can explain what happened."

Ashlyn glanced down at her nakedness. "I'm a bit underdressed for a meeting."

Kepler grinned. "How about we wear fur?"

Her wolf wriggled, excited to come out and run alongside Kepler's animal. But Ashlyn's chest felt tight. She was still uncertain. "You think that's the best way?"

"I want them to see, smell, and hear your wolf.

None of this questioning what you are bullshit, regardless of how you came to be. Plus, we can travel faster as wolves."

At least out here in the woods, she wasn't likely to attack someone's pet. And she had to learn to let her wolf out or they'd both go crazy. She nodded and took a deep breath. "Let me shift first, in case I have trouble."

"Go ahead." He nodded in encouragement, his eyes bright as stars. "I can't wait to run with you."

Closing her eyes, she let down the barriers she'd erected to contain her wolf. The animal swelled within her, a prickle of magic racing along Ashlyn's skin. This was so amazing, so exciting. She couldn't wait to see the world as her wolf again.

The scent of ash enveloped her, followed by a sudden headache. Her wolf no longer pressed at her awareness. Ashlyn scrunched her lids harder. *Wolf?* The image of her animal in shackles came to her, pale fur lit by abrasive, shifting colors.

Then a laugh like a roll of thunder filled her head.

CHAPTER THIRTEEN

Kepler watched Ashlyn's forehead crease in concentration and told himself to be patient. She'd done an amazing job containing the Alpha wolf inside her, but releasing it, embracing it, was new to her. It might take more effort.

Another minute passed. He frowned. "Ashlyn, is everything okay?"

Her eyes popped open, flashing purple light before settling to normal, human blue. "I'm fine."

Purple? He frowned. "What's wrong?"

"Nothing," her voice emerged husky, like it wasn't her own. "But my wolf doesn't want to shift right now. She wants us to talk."

He looked into her eyes, trying to understand her abrupt change of behavior. *We can talk in wolf form.*

Kepler? Help! Ashlyn's voice sounded far away.

He shook his head. *Ashlyn? What's going on?*

I don't know. I don't know where I am. The panic in her voice made his pulse race.

He pulled in a breath, staring at what appeared to be his mate smiling at him. The corrosive stink like burning coal had returned in force. He didn't know much about the creatures Darcy'd said might come through the hellmouth, but he knew this wasn't Ashlyn. She was possessed. Was it a demon? He'd have to play along until he came up with a plan or Ashlyn regained control.

The thing looked downward as if realizing it was naked. "Let's get accustomed to each other's human forms first."

In his head, he urged the real Ashlyn to take back control while out loud he said, "Of course. Why don't we find some clothes?"

"It *is* a bit chilly out here." Seemingly unaware Ashlyn was in communication with him, the demon stepped forward and placed a palm flat against his chest. Its veins seemed to glow through its skin with a faint, purplish light. "But you have a way of warming me up."

Trying not to gape, he covered its hand with his own. "I, um, need a little recovery time first."

The demon must've detected his distaste. Its eyes flashed purple again and narrowed. "You're smarter than I expected, especially for a beast."

Kepler bared his teeth and took a firm grip on the

creature's elbow. "What the fuck are you and where's my mate?"

"I'm your new master." A smile twisted not-Ashlyn's mouth. "You should be honored to be my consort."

A consort? That must be why the thing hadn't yet run away or tried to kill him. It must need him for some reason. He shook his head and gripped its elbow harder, which seemed to excite the demon because it rubbed Ashlyn's nipples against his arm. "I am delighted by this body's response to you."

Her body shuddered and, with a force that caught him off guard, ripped away from his grip. Hands balled into fists, Ashlyn pressed them against her temples. "Keep your hands off my mate."

Anger roiled through Ashlyn. How dare that thing possessing her body touch her mate with such familiarity! With fury fueling her, she screamed her protest, resuming control of her senses. The pain of twigs and stones dug into her knees. Then what felt like an electric jolt stole her breath and she lost sensation again.

Ashlyn strained against the pressure that had squeezed her into a remote corner of her own consciousness. *How can I be kicked out of my own body?* Her wolf had shoved her aside the few times the beast had taken control, but not like this. She had no hold on her limbs or voice, and her view of Kepler was small and fuzzy.

The sound of his words came to her through a muted roar, as if she was hearing it from behind a waterfall. "Ashlyn, are you in there? Use your wolf! Fight! Push the demon out!"

A demon? Weren't demons supposed to need an invitation? Or was that vampires? She couldn't remember. Straining against the pressure holding her, she shouted, *Get out!*

A voice responded to her, tone full of disdain. *I am no mere demon. Your kind call me an agathion. It is pointless to fight, so stop struggling. We will have a lot more fun if you cooperate.*

She had to make this thing leave. Where was her wolf? Changing tactics, she searched for her animal, but the demon possessing her had transplanted it. *What did you do to my wolf?*

The demon didn't answer. Instead, it seemed to be occupied fending off Kepler's attempt to tackle her. Through her fuzzy view, she watched her body raise both hands and send twin arcs of lightning against Kepler's chest.

He flew backward, landing on his back on the forest floor where he lay unmoving against the crushed branches.

Was he dead? Panic surged through her, and she flexed, straining against the agathion's hold on her.

Her body advanced on Kepler. "I'd hoped to savor

my first soul slowly, but perhaps a full meal is a better way to begin my sojourn on Earth."

Ashlyn didn't know what that meant, but it sounded bad. *Kepler, wake up!*

The agathion straddled her mate's body, splaying both hands against Kepler's chest. A trickle of pleasure washed into Ashlyn, not her own, but the agathion's as Kepler's perfect, golden energy flowed into it. "This male's life force is strong." The voice had become giddy. "Such ambrosia."

Kepler was defenseless. She had to do something. With a great burst of effort, she broke through the containment. Regained control. Stared down into her mate's shocked face.

He bared his teeth and golden sparks filled the air as Kepler's huge gray timber wolf materialized beneath her. Thrashing, he bucked her off, sending her sprawling on the forest floor.

In her head, the thunderous voice shouted, *Enough!* and a flash of purple light blinded her. Kepler and the world around her disappeared into a roiling mass of colors and shapes.

An angular face the size of a bus loomed above her, reminding her of the *Wizard of Oz*. But her sense of humor fizzled as the agathion spoke, revealing wickedly angular teeth. "I suggest you settle down and be quiet." Its lavender eyes flashed like sheet lightning. "You wouldn't want to alert the others to your presence."

The way it said *others* made her shudder. She glanced around, still unable to make sense of her surroundings. "What others? Where am I?"

"Stupid human. So unaware. So helplessly bound to your own mundane plane of existence." The face loomed closer, kicking up a gust that smelled like singed hair. "Let's just say you don't want the beings passing through that realm taking an interest in a stranded mortal soul."

Ashlyn shrank back, trying to make the billowing colors around her solidify into recognizable objects or spaces. She felt like a kite being tossed in the wind, vertigo making her dizzy. Strange pinging and warbling noises surrounded her that seemed to have no source. The only stable thing she had was the thread connecting her to Kepler. *Kepler, are you all right?*

She could feel his confusion as he answered, *I got away. What is going on?*

That thing's called an agathion. It tried to eat your soul. Ashlyn's throat felt tight. *I can't beat it. It kicked me out of my own body.*

I'm going for help.

Ashlyn knew what needed to happen. The monster controlling her body had to be killed. *She* had to be killed. *You have to kill me before I hurt anyone else.*

No, the witches did this to you. They might know what to do.

There's no time. This monster can't be allowed to reach the town.

She could feel his angst through their connection, as she was certain he could feel hers. They'd just found each other, just discovered forever, and their chance at a future was being ripped away. But there was no other option. *Promise me, Kepler.*

After a brief pause, he said, *I promise I won't let you hurt any more people.*

That was all she could ask for. Closing her eyes, she thought about her wolf. Had the agathion killed her? She remembered seeing the animal in shackles, so maybe it was still alive. *Wolf, where are you?*

A mournful howl floated above the other strange sounds. Off balance, she tried to move toward it. If she focused on thoughts of her wolf, her surroundings seemed a little more solid. The ground became what felt like rough stone, but the world—realm, the agathion had called it—made little sense to her. All of her senses seemed jumbled, what should be something she saw coming across as a taste or smell, and her sense of touch would sometimes translate as a color or sound. At least she hadn't encountered any other monsters.

Yet.

She pushed through what felt like yellow foam and paused at what looked like a vibrating tightrope over what could've been a river of magma. Her wolf called to her from the other side. Touching the tightrope with her toes, she was filled by the flavor of chocolate. *What the hell.* She felt like she was playing a child's board game gone horribly wrong.

Crossing over with more ease than expected, she was stopped by a bouncing green orb. Watching it made her eyes cross, so she closed them and kept going. Then the scent of anise brushed by her. She felt it pause and reverse direction toward her again. Something about it made her blood run cold, as if she'd gained the attention of something. Her wolf howled again, a snarling, protective sound, and she started to run.

Behind her, she could feel the anise scent approaching. *Shit shit shit. What is it?*

Ahead, a periwinkle sliver of light held steady amidst the rest of the shifting landscape. Her wolf's howl was coming from in there, calling her. She dove for it, the brush of anise at her heels, and everything went dark.

For a moment, she lay very still, unsure what had happened. Am I still alive?

A soft whine reached her, and she lifted her head to find a pair of glowing blue eyes watching her in the darkness.

"Wolf!" Ashlyn's voice echoed back at her, as if she was inside a vast cavern. She crawled forward over hard, rocky ground. "You're all right."

A long pink tongue met her cheek.

Hope warmed in Ashlyn's chest. Perhaps together they'd be strong enough to force the agathion from her body. Assuming Kepler hadn't killed her yet. Certainly she'd feel something when and if he did? She had to assume her body was still alive until then.

Wrapping her arms around the wolf's furry neck, she hugged her tightly. "I'm glad you're alive. Ready to help me fight a monster?"

Her wolf nuzzled her ear and whined softly.

Ashlyn ran her hands over what felt like a solid ring forged in one piece around the wolf's throat. It was connected by a thick chain bolted to the cave's wall. The only light in the cavern seemed to come from her wolf's eyes, but she saw what might be a keyhole embedded in a metal plate where the chain connected to the wall.

Remembering how Kepler had picked the lock to her front door, she reached out to him. *Kepler, can you hear me?*

He didn't answer. Her nausea returned, not vertigo this time, but dread. Had the agathion got him? Maybe it was just the cave blocking reception. She scanned their surroundings, hoping to see a door. A key. A magic button that said 'eject.' Anything.

But the surrounding blackness seemed absolute.

The wolf bent and lifted something in its jaws, depositing it in Ashlyn's lap. The thing moved.

Ashlyn recoiled, ready to shove it off, but a protective sensation washed through her from her wolf. In the dim glow from her wolf's eyes, a mangy, one-eyed ferret stared up at her. The tiny creature cowered in her lap as if expecting a blow.

"Oh, you poor thing," said Ashlyn. "Are you trapped here, too?"

The ferret nodded.

Ashlyn hadn't expected the creature to answer, but then her wolf wasn't an ordinary wolf, so she shouldn't be surprised. "Are you a shifter animal?"

The ferret shook its head no.

"Do you know the way out?"

The creature jerked its head to the right in a purposeful way, as if telling her to look over there. Then it hopped off her lap and scratched her thigh with its front feet.

Fingers buried in her wolf's ruff, Ashlyn said, "I think it wants me to go with it."

Her wolf nudged her shoulder.

Stomach churning, she rose. The ferret ran a few steps away, all but disappearing in the darkness before it turned to face her, single eye glittering like a dim star.

Ashlyn followed the ferret's hunched gait, walking carefully over the uneven stone. She had no idea how the thing knew where it was going, but it stayed only a few paces away, turning to face her every few steps. Ahead, what looked like a glowing orange circle grew brighter, eventually clarifying into what looked like a group of knee-high mushrooms.

The ferret stopped at the outer edge and stood on its hind legs, peering over the caps.

Something about the circle made her head spin. "Curiouser and curiouser. What is it? A fairy circle?"

The ferret scurried around the circumference, coming to stop at her other side. It once more stood on its hind legs to peer into the middle.

"You want me to go in there?" The idea made Ashlyn want to vomit.

The ferret scratched the top of her foot like it had her thigh.

"I guess that means yes." Sighing, Ashlyn looked over her shoulder. She could no longer see her wolf, but she could feel her comforting presence. Stepping into the circle of mushrooms might very well send Ashlyn to yet another place. What if she couldn't get back?

The ferret scratched at her foot again.

Bending, Ashlyn picked the creature up. Its fur was softer than she'd expected, its body light and bony. It squeaked as if in pain. She hadn't been rough, but adjusted her grip. "I'm not going to hurt you, but I need you to come with me."

The ferret lowered its head in what might have been resignation.

Steeling herself, Ashlyn lifted a foot and stepped into the circle.

CHAPTER FOURTEEN

𝒩o way in hell would Kepler let Ashlyn die. A witch had caused this, and a witch was going to fix it. He'd accept nothing less. He dodged trees and leaped over brush, heading straight toward the coven's gate. *Ashlyn, what's your witch friend's name?*

She didn't answer.

He slowed, searching for their mental bond. But there was nothing. Dread settled into his gut. Darcy's warning about monsters hovering around the hellmouth returned to haunt him. Ashlyn was alone on the other side. He glanced in the direction he'd come from, realizing he'd also abandoned her body to a monster. An agathion, she'd called it. *It was leave her or kill her.* He prayed the witches knew what an agathion was. Raising his muzzle, he howled in frustration but continued onward.

Despite his natural healing power, his chest still

burned where the demon had touched him. He'd never felt as close to death as in that moment. If his wolf hadn't taken over, he was certain he'd be dead right now. No one the agathion came in contact with stood a chance. More was at stake than the life of his mate.

He reached the wrought-iron fence and skirted it toward the gated driveway, praying the witches had a way to exorcize the thing without hurting Ashlyn. *I should've let Darcy introduce me to the coven.* He hadn't met the local witches and had no idea if they were friendly to shifters or not. Ashlyn seemed to think they wanted to help, but he'd feel better if he had backup.

Cal, can you hear me? Desperate, he searched for the connection they'd shared earlier. *I need your help.*

Relief flooded him when Cal answered, *Glad you've come to your senses. What happened?*

Ashlyn tried to shift, but something went wrong. I think a demon came through instead of her wolf.

Fuck, man. Okay. Finch and I are almost there.

The last person Kepler expected Cal to rally was the grizzly shifter. *What about the pack?*

I thought about what you said, and you're right. We need level heads here. Plus, I'm following chain of command. Which actually meant he wanted to show off for the Regional Director. But before Kepler could comment, Cal's voice grew more serious. *What the hell is that stench?*

Shit. Kepler suddenly realized Cal was probably backtracking his trail, which put him on a collision course with the demon. *Stop. It's the demon. Don't go back to where you left me and Ashlyn. Come to the coven house.*

The witches? Aren't they the ones who started all this?

I don't think it was these witches. But I'm hoping they have a way to get rid of the demon. Kepler shifted to human form and approached the keypad. *Whatever you do, stay away from Ashlyn until we have the witches on our side.*

Fuck, man, she'd better be worth it.

She is. He reached for the buzzer, but the gate swung open before he touched it. Of course the witches were waiting for him. Aware he was naked as a jaybird, he strode down the driveway, keeping his wolf at the surface in case he needed a quick change.

A group of women waited for him on the porch of a big gray house. One of them hurried forward with a fleece blanket, her gaze seemingly unable to stay off his junk. She flushed as he accepted the blanket, then stepped aside. He wrapped it around his waist and stared up at the coven. "You were expecting me."

An older witch at the front of the group nodded, her face stern. "Saw you on the gate camera when you ran away the first time. My name's Tessa. I lead this coven." Her attention moved past him toward the gate which had swung closed behind him. "Where are the other two?"

"Cal went to get the pack." He decided it might be best if they thought he had a lot of backup on the way.

"But Ashlyn, my mate, seems to have been possessed by a demon."

Exclamations of distress rose from the group of witches. "We're too late."

"The agathion is loose?"

"This is a disaster."

Tessa raised a hand, and the voices silenced. "Thank you for bringing this to our attention. You may remain inside the compound for safety. We will take it from here."

Kepler put his hands on his hips. "I don't think so. That's my mate you're talking about."

Once more, the group murmured. The older witch raised her brows. "The woman or the man?"

"The woman, Ashlyn."

"Are you certain? She isn't one of your kind."

"Of course I'm certain." He hated the way supernaturals always divided people by bloodlines. If it wasn't pack versus pack, it was wolf versus bear, or shifter versus witch. He was done with it. "One of your kind cursed her, so I expect one of you can reverse it."

She shook her head, gaze full of regret. "We have apprehended the guilty party and she will pay, I promise. But there is no way to reverse the spell. We must destroy the host before the demon gets any stronger."

A dark-haired witch shouldered forward, glaring at the coven leader. "She's more than a host. Her name's

Ashlyn, and she's my friend. I feel partially responsible for what's happened to her."

"It was in no way your fault," Tessa insisted.

"I invited Jen to visit." Muffy tapped her own chest. "I invited them both to my party. All of this happened right under my nose. I'm a terrible witch and a terrible sister. I should've seen it."

"Your sister is the witch who's been creating the rogues?" Kepler asked, his hands balling into fists at his sides. His wolf was ready to rip out someone's throat. *We need them alive to reverse the spell on Ashlyn*, he reminded his animal. "Can she reverse the hex on Ashlyn?"

Tessa glared at Muffy. "You reveal too much, especially to someone outside the coven. There's nothing Jen or any of us can do."

Muffy threw up her arms. "She wants to make this right. But you won't talk to her."

"Her suggestions are all forbidden magic," Tessa said.

Kepler advanced up the steps, forcing several witches to stumble backward as he put himself nose-to-nose with Tessa. "Let me talk to the witch who did this."

Beside the coven leader, Muffy held her ground. "It's his business, too. They're mates. I know I'd want Jonathan to do everything he could if I was in trouble."

Tessa shook her head, gaze moving between Kepler and Muffy. "Impossible."

"The witch who summoned the agathion must know its weakness," Kepler pressed. "I want to talk to her."

The front door opened and a blonde woman called out, "Tessa, there's a shifter at the gate who says he's with the State Troopers. What do you want me to do?"

Tessa rolled her eyes. "I had hoped to settle this problem internally, but I see it's already spread beyond the coven's boundaries. Let him in."

Moments later, Finch and Cal stood at Kepler's side, both naked. Finch spoke low, hands discreetly over his crotch and eyes on Tessa. "Afraid I don't have my credentials on me at the moment, ma'am."

"We have other means of verifying your identity, Director Finch." Her gaze remained shrewdly on his face, although the younger witches around her were obviously ogling the naked men. Tessa turned toward the house. "Follow me, please."

Inside, Cal and Finch were given blankets like Kepler's then they all followed Tessa to a low door. The witch looked over her shoulder. "My Circle of Protection was damaged, and this makeshift one is fragile. Please do not disturb or pass over the stones."

She descended a narrow stairway into a basement that was barely more than a crawlspace. Kepler had to duck to keep from bumping his head on the bare joists overhead, and though the space appeared dry, the air smelled earthy and pungent, like mushrooms. A few bare lightbulbs hung at regular intervals down the joists, revealing a circle of stones on top of clear plastic vapor barrier. In the center sat a woman on a wooden chair.

Kepler'd expected her to be tied up or something, but her hands rested in her lap, clutching a wad of tissues. She lifted her chin to regard the approaching group. Her long auburn tresses hung limp around her ghostly pale face, and her reddened eyes looked as if she'd been crying.

Muffy hurried forward, stopping short at the edge of the stones. "Jen, the agathion—"

"I know. Hamilton told me."

Kepler frowned. "Who's Hamilton?" He hadn't seen any male witches since he'd arrived.

"Jen's familiar." Muffy faced him, eyes worried. "The agathion was holding him hostage, forcing her—"

"Muffy," Tessa's tone held warning.

Muffy nodded, stepping back to allow the others to approach. Cal hung back, eyes wide, but Finch moved forward next to Kepler.

Stopping only when his bare toes nearly touched the stone circle, Kepler glared at the witch inside. Finally, he stood face-to-face with the person who'd started everything. Who'd evaded him for years. He had so many questions. None of them mattered now except for one. "How do I banish the agathion?"

Finch planted ham-sized fists on his hips. "And why are you suddenly helping?"

Jen shook her head, mouth a grim line. "He

kidnapped my familiar and broke his promise to give him back to me after I completed the hex." She looked past the shifters toward the coven leader. "But I can't banish the agathion back to his realm because it would require me to use forbidden magic."

Tessa's arms were crossed, her face stern. "The magic is forbidden for a reason. It opens a hellmouth. Anything could come through. Besides, even if I let you try, you don't have the proper components."

"If it's the only way to get Ashlyn back, we need to do it," Kepler said and looked at Jen again. "What components? Tell me what you need and I'll get it."

"I need a physical sample from the being to be hexed. Blood, skin, hair."

"That's easy." Kepler exhaled with relief. "I'll go to Ashlyn's apartment and bring you her comb, toothbrush, whatever you need."

Jen shook her head. "Old samples won't work. We need samples from the body while it's inhabited."

Tessa added, "The agathion knows that. Even if it didn't kill you on sight, it won't allow you to collect materials that will banish it."

Kepler grit his teeth, recalling Ashlyn's glowing purple veins and how close he'd come to death when the agathion had touched him. But he refused to give up. "I think I can get close enough. It called me its consort when I was with it earlier."

Jen blinked, horror filling her eyes. "You're Ashlyn's mate?"

"Yes." He felt his lip curl in a snarl, exposing one long canine.

She visibly swallowed. "Then it may allow you near, at least for a time. The problem will be when you try to get away."

Kepler grimaced and nodded, one hand going to his chest to touch the tender scars the creature had left there. "Maybe I shouldn't try to get away. Is there some way you can have everything ready to go so I can finish the spell right there?"

Her eyes grew thoughtful. "We do have more of the glass with her wolf's blood on it. If I construct a blade, and you mingle their blood—"

"The host is human," Tessa interrupted. "She doesn't have the experience or knowledge to respond to an open hellmouth. We can't take a chance that something worse than the agathion will come through."

Kepler wasn't sure who he hated more, Jen for hexing Ashlyn, or Tessa for hindering the only means of saving her. "Ashlyn's wolf is an Alpha. She'll know what to do."

Tessa looked at him with pity. "In order to cast the spell that let the agathion through in the first place, Jen bound the wolf. Ashlyn is on her own."

His heart sank as he thought of Ashlyn all by herself on the other side. What if Ashlyn was already dead? *Ashlyn, please respond.* He tried to summon their mental bond again.

No response.

Even so, he insisted, "Ashlyn's smart. She'll know to come through when she sees it."

Annoyingly calm, Jen replied, "She may be able to free her wolf. Hamilton's helping her now."

The pinprick of hope was all Kepler needed. He turned to Tessa. "We have to try."

Tessa shook her head. "And if we fail?"

He looked first at Finch, who nodded, then at Cal, who looked a little unwell but nodded, too. They knew the stakes. They knew what had to be done.

Fighting back the chill trying to paralyze his bones, Kepler said, "If we fail, we kill her."

*A*shlyn stepped over the mushrooms into the circle, holding her breath in anticipation. The next thing she knew, she stood in what looked like a study. *I was right, that was a portal.* Looking behind her, she was relieved to see an open wooden door that revealed only blackness. *That must be the opening I just stepped through.* This place was so weird.

The room held a closed roll-top desk, a rickety wooden chair, and bookshelves, everything in sight a monochrome shade of orange. But what struck her most were what had to be a hundred mounted taxidermy heads on every spare inch of wall space. Some appeared to be common animals from Earth plus a few that appeared to be human, but others had grotesque horned protrusions, extra eyes, or double rows of teeth.

She cradled the ferret against her chest like a teddy bear. "What am I supposed to do in here?"

It wriggled to be free, so she set it on the floor. It loped toward the chair and jumped from it to a bookshelf and began to climb. Was this where the demon that possessed her body lived? She moved toward the desk, but her steps faltered as she caught sight of the head of a man mounted to the wall. His curly hair and contorted expression was familiar. *The shifter who attacked me in the alley.* She wanted to be sick.

The ferret latched onto a book, tipping it from its slot on a high shelf, and Ashlyn forced her gaze away from the menagerie of heads to help pull the book free. In the weird orange light, it looked almost red, and the cover felt velvety yet slick at the same time. Her gut churned thinking about what it might be made of. No writing or images decorated the front or thin spine.

Opening it, she discovered its pages were also blank. A smell like oatmeal wafted upward, and as she turned the pages, the smell changed to diesel fumes, strawberries, campfire... Each page had a smell instead of words. She frowned and looked up at the ferret. "What is this?"

It scurried back along the bookshelf and hopped to the top of the desk cabinet, scratching at the closed roll-top.

Ashlyn shut the book and moved to the desk. The tambour moved smoothly as she slid it up, revealing a desktop that looked more like a surgeon's table, with bloody instruments laid out in a neat row. Appalled, she drew back.

The ferret nudged a scalpel and looked at her.

"What do you want me to do with that?" Ashlyn glanced at the heads staring blankly into the room. No way was she removing body parts from anyone or anything.

Standing on its hind legs, the ferret used a front paw to point at the book still clutched in her hand.

"Oh, you want me to cut up the book?" Destroying the nasty thing felt right. She swiped aside the medical instruments and set the book on the desk. Picking up the scalpel, she poised it over the cover.

The ferret lunged forward and nipped her wrist.

"Ow! Why'd you do that?"

It clawed the book open, riffling pages until the book fell on one that smelled familiar. Wildflowers. Honey. *Wolf.*

Her eyes widened. "My wolf?"

With one small claw, the ferret made a cutting motion along the bound edge of the page.

Ashlyn looked from the scalpel to the page. "Cut the page out?"

The ferret backed away.

"All right…" Licking her lips, she took a breath and placed the scalpel against the page. When the ferret didn't object, she sliced the page free.

She'd expected to feel something, see something, but the page just sat there. "Now what?"

The ferret pushed the page toward her, so she picked it up. Then it hopped off the desk and ran back to the door, where it turned around to look at her expectantly. Okay, she was supposed to follow it again. Wrapping the page around the scalpel, she clutched them both in one fist.

Then she thought of something. "What about you? Is there something in here that can help you?"

The ferret shook its head and edged closer to the opening.

Feeling sorry for the tiny creature, she picked it up. This time, it didn't flinch. The blackness beyond the door was daunting, but she knew her wolf was on the other side waiting. With a final glance at the strange room, she stepped through, once more finding herself at the edge of the mushroom circle.

"Wolf, I'm coming!" she cried.

Somewhere in the darkness, her wolf whined, and she followed the sound until she could see its blue glowing eyes. At her animal's side once more, she set the ferret down and knelt on the stone floor. "I got this."

She unwrapped the page, keeping the scalpel in her other hand. Except the page was no longer a paper. It was a leaf with a long, serrated stem. *Not a stem*. She turned to the ferret. "A key."

The ferret nodded, front feet pressed against the wall where the chain was connected.

"I feel like Alice in Wonderland," she muttered and placed the key into the keyhole on the wall. "Here goes nothing."

Color exploded all around her. The scalpel fell from her grip and she closed her eyes against a sudden return of vertigo, groping blindly for her wolf. "Wolf? Wolf, where are you?"

Her wolf pressed against her, body warm and solid in the ethereal surroundings. Clinging to the animal's thick ruff, she knelt, feeling warm and giddy with success. "We did it!"

She cracked open one eye, focusing on her wolf and allowing the billowing colors to flow past her. Her elation faded a little. "We're still not in my body."

Small paws touched her leg, and she slid her gaze down to find the ferret looking up at her. In the colored light, it looked even more abused, the reddish fur patchy in places and the missing eye crusted with scar tissue. Trembling, the ferret climbed onto her lap and curled itself into a ball.

A scent like anise grew stronger, and Ashlyn's entire being prickled with awareness as she remembered how it had pursued her earlier. Was it one of the monsters the agathion had warned her about? She searched the ground around her for the dropped scalpel, but it was nowhere in sight.

Her wolf leaned against her, muscles tense and

wary. Ashlyn felt like a rabbit caught in the open. She had no option but to remain perfectly still and hope whatever it was passed her over.

After the smell faded, she whispered, "Do you know what that was?"

Of course the animals couldn't answer. But they both stayed close, as if she held the power to shield them from danger. Longing for Kepler, she closed her eyes and pictured him, strong and protective. She imagined his arms around her and the warm masculine scent of his body when he held her close. *Kepler, what do I do?*

Ashlyn, I knew you were alive! Kepler's voice flooded her with relief.

We're still connected!

Of course. You're my mate.

She wished she could fall into his arms. *I freed my wolf, but I have no idea where I am or what to do next.*

Can you sense your body? We need to know where it is.

Her chest tightened. *No, I'm completely disconnected.*

That's okay. We can follow your scent. The witches have come up with a plan to get you back into your body, Kepler said. *Watch for the hellmouth. When you see it, don't hesitate, go through it.*

She tried to remember what she'd seen when the agathion had thrust her out of her body, but she'd been so confused. *I don't know what it looks like.*

I'll tell you when, but if we lose connection again, trust your wolf. Follow her lead. He hesitated, as if uncertain what to say next. *And Ashlyn? Forgive me.*

For what?

Breaking the curse is going to hurt.

Kepler rode the four-wheeler hard, losing sight of Cal's russet fur as he rerouted to avoid a fallen tree. He couldn't carry the glass knife Jen had made while he was in wolf form, and he couldn't easily track the agathion in human form, so they'd settled on letting Cal sniff out the trail. Kepler wore an old flannel jacket the witches had given him, along with a pair of cargo pants that were one size too small, the hexed knife hidden in the pocket on his thigh.

In Kepler's head, Cal said, *I think we're getting close.*

Do not let it spot you, Kepler warned for what felt like the hundredth time. He nudged Ashlyn. *We're almost there. Be ready.*

Okay. Her voice trembled.

He was about to reassure her when Cal interrupted, *Shit. It's almost to the highway.*

They had to stop it before it reached civilization. A naked woman asking for help on the side of the road would immediately attract attention, and they wanted to keep this as quiet as possible. Kepler gunned the ATV. One of his wheels caught air, and he leaned into it to keep the vehicle upright, landing hard, wheels churning up leaves and dirt behind him.

Between the gray trees far ahead, he spotted a flash of pink and blue hair. *I've got her, Cal. Pull back.*

Good luck. Cal slowed to a trot, allowing Kepler to whip past. *We're ready if you need us.*

Kepler's stomach clenched. They had to end the monster, one way or another, and if the plan didn't work or something happened to Kepler before he could complete it, Cal and Finch would move in and kill the vessel. Kill Ashlyn. Kepler wasn't about to let that happen.

"Ashlyn!" he yelled over the roar of his engine, hoping to stall the agathion before it reached the road.

The pink and blue hair stopped, and the figure turned to face him, blue eyes flashing purple. He pulled up just out of reach, letting the engine fall to an idle. The agathion cocked its head. "You surprise me, shifter."

"I thought about what you said, about being your consort." Kepler's heart thundered against his ribs and made it hard to keep his voice steady. "You're obviously powerful. Humans will fall at your feet and worship you in terror. So, I agree."

A grin split its mouth, and Kepler fought to keep the revulsion off his face as it stepped toward him. "Do you know what a consort does? What will be required of you?"

"I understand what being a consort means." The

witches had discussed this in detail, directing Kepler on exactly what the agathion was likely to crave, including tastes of his soul. But if that's what it took to get close enough to save Ashlyn, Kepler was ready. Still, he wanted to offer other alternatives first. The monster was restrained to human limitations while inhabiting a mortal body. It had to be tired and cold.

"But first let's give you comfort." Kepler gestured to its naked, scratched up skin. *Ashlyn's skin*, Kepler thought, examining the twigs and leaves snarled in its long pink and blue hair. Its bare, dirty feet were also smudged with blood. "I can provide clothes, accommodations, transport, food. Whatever you desire."

The agathion took another step toward him. "Your mate is no longer in this body, if that's what you're worried about. She's dead. Even if I decide I'm done with this realm, this body will be a corpse."

Kepler pressed his lips together. The agathion must not know Kepler was still in contact with Ashlyn and that her soul was alive. Alive and ready to fight back. He nodded deferentially. "I understand. You're stronger than she was." God, he hated saying that. He shrugged. "That makes *you* my mate, now."

As if acknowledging a victory, the agathion lifted its chin. "It's good you recognize that. I accept your service." It shifted its gaze to the ATV. "What is this transport you have brought me?"

Things were proceeding better than Kepler'd

expected. Sliding back on the seat to make room, he gestured to the handlebars. "A four-wheeler. I'll show you how to drive."

If the agathion was occupied steering the ATV, Kepler could use Jen's knife. The blade was nothing more than a shard of glass no bigger than his thumb with a wad of duct tape for a handle, but it had to be embedded in the body in a place it could not be dislodged, at least not until Ashlyn regained control. Once she did, he'd remove the dagger, shatter it, and break the agathion's power over her.

The agathion waved him back toward the driver's spot. "You shall transport me."

Shit. Kepler felt his eye twitch and hoped the agathion didn't notice. He should've known things wouldn't be easy. *Time for Plan B.*

Instead of sliding forward, he dismounted and went to the back of the vehicle where a tote had been strapped to the rack. "Let's get you clothes first. You must be cold. It'll be even colder riding the wheeler."

Swaggering forward, the agathion put both palms against Kepler's flanks, pressing itself against him from behind. "I believe humans have many methods of keeping warm."

Skin crawling, Kepler remained steady. He couldn't disengage without making the agathion doubt him. "I look forward to showing you many human pleasures once we've reached the comfort of my house." He pulled open the tote and removed a white cashmere sweater one of the witches had donated. "Right now, you'll enjoy these clothes. I promise."

The agathion frowned and looked past him to the tote. "Where did you acquire these things?"

Kepler shrugged, trying to remain nonchalant. His heartbeat pounded in his ears. "Stole them. There are plenty of homesteads in these parts that don't lock their doors."

To his relief, that seemed to satisfy the agathion. It took the sweater and held it against its chest. "What else have you brought me?"

Kepler reached for the knife in his pocket. He had to strike just right, or he'd kill rather than incapacitate. When the agathion leaned over to rummage through the clothing, Kepler struck. He angled the blade into the agathion's back, sliding along ribs until the glass shard lay beneath the skin like a splinter.

The agathion screamed, body contorting. It tried to remove the blade, but the handle was out of reach. Blood welled around the embedded hilt, trickling down the amber skin.

Now, Ashlyn! Come through now!

Crimson light filled the air, and all of a sudden, a small reddish ferret popped into existence. It tumbled across the ground and came to rest at the base of a tree, immediately righting itself and scurrying out of sight. He'd been prepared for monsters, but a ferret? He called to Cal, "One of you catch that thing."

It's that witch's familiar, Cal replied. *Let it go.* The

russet wolf and Finch in his huge grizzly form had emerged from the underbrush.

Hell, no, Finch said and shot off into the trees. *The witch betrayed us.*

Kepler didn't have time to wonder that he could now hear Finch. The agathion had turned to focus on him, purple lightning arching from its fingertips. "Traitor! You will pay!"

Dodging the bolt, Kepler called, *Ashlyn, where are you?*

Had the witch betrayed them? Had this all been a ploy to get her familiar back? If Ashlyn couldn't get control of her body, he knew what had to happen next. He'd promised. But he didn't want Cal and Finch to touch her. Ashlyn was his. His love. His life. His responsibility. Heart breaking, he prepared to shift into his wolf.

Just as Ashlyn's body collapsed to the forest floor.

CHAPTER SIXTEEN

What felt like a hurricane struck Ashlyn, shredding the surrounding colors into jagged pieces and making it impossible to breathe. Kepler's voice reached her just as the smell of ash bowled her over, breaking her hold on her wolf. She tumbled end over end, dizziness intensifying until she could no longer tell up from down.

By pure force of will, she stopped her momentum and got back on her feet. Ferocious snarling drew her attention to where her wolf was locked in combat with the figure of a man. Purple lightning danced across his skin. *The agathion!* The hellmouth must've opened, but nothing around her looked like a portal.

Scrambling forward, she waited for an opportunity to jump in and help her wolf, but the fight was too chaotic. She was afraid she might do more harm than good. Her wolf's teeth and claws cut into the agathion, and he returned damage with arcs of light. She couldn't tell who was winning.

Behind her, she heard her name. Turning, she spotted a dot of gold no bigger than her thumb. It remained steady while the world around it churned. Through it, Kepler's nearness was a lifeline, drawing her toward him. The hellmouth.

Kepler, the agathion is fighting my wolf!

You need to come through now! he urged.

The agathion had her wolf by the throat. Ashlyn clenched her fists. Short of throwing random punches, she was helpless. *I can't leave her!*

The sound of the storm shifted, becoming more like sighing. The anise smell that had stalked her earlier returned. Terror spiked through her. Where was the ferret? Had something got it while she wasn't watching? *Kepler, there's something else here,* she sent. *I think it's hunting me.*

Come through now. His voice held the same tone of command he'd used when she'd first met him, his Alpha tone, and she could feel his desperation through their bond. *Ashlyn, please.*

A second anise scent, slightly sharper, joined the first. *Oh, God.* A pack? She still couldn't see anything. Shadows flickered between her and the gold dot. What happened if the beings that smelled like anise reached the portal first?

Wolf, hurry!

Her wolf stood on top of the agathion, teeth in its

throat. For a moment, she thought they'd won. But then her wolf's eyes met hers, and a single word reached her. *Go.*

The agathion thrust a hand against the wolf's chest, sending it flying. Then he raised both hands toward her. Lightning shot out, but her wolf pounced, sending the bolts astray.

Go, the wolf sent again.

The portal would soon be closed, with or without her. Ashlyn had to go without her wolf. She backed a step toward the hellmouth. Then another. Her wolf was holding the agathion off. Giving Ashlyn a chance to escape. But what would happen to her wolf once Ashlyn left? The animal had become more a part of her than she'd ever imagined possible.

Lightning crackled through the air, and two more things that looked like men popped into view. They were bigger than the agathion, and their skin glittered with what looked like a million stars. Turning purple glowing eyes toward her and the hellmouth, they ignored the fight and moved forward. Her wolf howled, begging her to go.

Chest tight, Ashlyn knew she was out of options. She had to leave.

Spinning, she dove for the portal.

She slammed back into her body with the force of a freight train. A rush of cool air met her lungs. Her cheek was pressed against the damp ground, yellow leaves filling her vision. The solid earth beneath her felt almost wrong in its steadiness, and the middle of her back was on fire. She turned her head and forced her eyes to focus, seeing her mate standing several feet away. She tried to say his name, but only managed a gasp.

He stayed back, eyes wary. "Ashlyn?"

"My wolf." Her throat spasmed, and her hands clawed at the damp leaves. "It's trying to kill my wolf."

A pained look fleeted across Kepler's face. "I'm sorry. We can't wait." Kneeling next to her, he yanked something out of her back.

It felt as if he'd just ripped every vein out of her body. She screamed in agony, stars filling her vision.

"Shit, that's a lot of blood," Kepler said, pressing hard against her back.

Through a haze of pain, she heard Cal ask, "Did it work?"

She heard the sound of crunching glass.

"Yes," Kepler growled.

She wanted to protest that it hadn't. That her wolf was still on the other side, fighting for her life. But pain was making it impossible to breathe, much less speak.

"So Jen didn't betray us." Cal sounded relieved.

Kepler muttered. "Fuck. Why isn't she healing?"

"Maybe it's not her," an unfamiliar voice said. "I have a bad feeling about this. Maybe the agathion's fooling us."

Her fingers and toes felt like ice, and her teeth chattered. *Why am I so cold?*

"It's her," Kepler's voice held an edge. "She said the agathion was trying to kill her wolf. If she lost her animal, she lost her ability to heal."

Ashlyn's heart cracked at those words. Kepler had been right about a shifter's animal being a part of them, and the emptiness she now felt hurt more than the pain in her back. Would she ever know if her wolf had won or lost?

"She was protecting me," Ashlyn whispered.

She couldn't feel the strength of her animal anymore. Couldn't feel much of anything. *Wolf, please come back.*

But as she drifted into unconsciousness, she was certain her wolf was gone.

The ATV ride was rougher than Kepler liked as he drove toward the road while holding Ashlyn limply in front of him. The wound on her back needed stitches, but shouldn't need a hospital, even for someone without shifter healing, but for some reason the bleeding wouldn't stop. He'd just reached the pavement when a truck pulled alongside his ATV.

Muffy was at the wheel and Tessa jumped out, flinging open the door to the back seat. "I thought you'd need help. Get in."

Kepler laid Ashlyn on the bench seat and climbed in beside her. Several blankets lay folded on the seat, and he pulled one haphazardly over his mate, trying to warm her. Her skin felt chilly and the blood on her bare skin had become tacky. "She won't stop bleeding. I think she's in shock."

Tessa closed the door and climbed back in front.

Muffy slammed the truck into gear and did a U-turn on the two-lane highway. Instead of buckling up, Tessa sat on her knees and leaned over the seat. "Let me see."

Cradling Ashlyn against his chest, Kepler allowed Tessa to examine the wound. Ashlyn's back glistened crimson, her matted hair stuck to her shoulders. The sharp metallic scent of her blood filled the cab, and he hated the way her eyelids fluttered, showing only the whites.

The witch made a noise in the back of her throat. "Did you puncture her lung?"

"No." Kepler knew he spoke too sharply, but he was furious. "I embedded it under her skin as you instructed. Please, do whatever it takes. Save her."

"I worried this might happen." Tessa dug into a bag on the seat beside her, bringing out some sort of poultice. She mashed some green gunk that smelled like astringent onto the bloody gash and taped a wide gauze pad over it. Then she placed her palm flat over the wound and spoke a few words in a strange language. "That should seal the wound."

"Is she going to be all right?" Kepler stroked Ashlyn's hair.

"I can't say yet. She's lost a lot of blood."

Muffy was driving them away from town, he realized, and suspicion rose in his chest. "Where are you going? We need to get her to a hospital."

"The agathion was stronger than we expected," Tessa said, eyebrows pinched. "If she can't beat it, we can't have her loose among humans."

He clutched Ashlyn tighter against his chest. "Then how do you plan to keep her alive?"

Tessa's glared at him. "I've stopped the bleeding. There is nothing more a doctor can do. She's best off in our care."

Kepler begrudgingly understood her reasoning, but it didn't make him any less angry. "I crushed the knife. You said crushing it would break the agathion's hold on her."

"That was our best guess, but none of us are overly familiar with this magic. No one practices it."

"Jen does." He gritted his teeth, thinking of the ferret running away like a coward. "She set us up. This was all so she could get her familiar back."

Muffy scowled over her shoulder at him. "Of course she hoped she'd get Hamilton back, but that wasn't her goal in the end."

"How do you know? That ferret was the first one through the hellmouth. Ashlyn almost didn't make it. Her wolf…" He couldn't finish. He couldn't imagine having his own wolf ripped from him. Was that why Ashlyn was dying?

Ashlyn's fingers moved against his chest, and he looked down to see her lips moving. Leaning close, he heard her say, "...ferret saved us."

He had no idea if she was delirious or actually conscious enough to be listening. He hoped it was the latter. But that gave his anger nowhere to go. He slumped against the seat, breathing in shallow, angry gasps.

"What is she saying?" Tessa asked.

"She says the ferret saved her," he snarled. "That damned familiar should've been the one to stay behind, not her wolf."

Tessa's eyes narrowed, then she turned around and buckled in. "I'll question Jen about that later. Right now, let's keep your mate alive."

CHAPTER SEVENTEEN

Ashlyn woke in an unfamiliar bed, sunlight glowing through gauzy curtains. She sat up, feeling weak, but alive. Yet there was an emptiness inside her. *Wolf?*

There was no response.

In a chair next to her, Kepler slumped to one side, mouth slightly open while he slept. Her hands and arms were covered in small scratches, as if she'd been rolling around in a briar patch, and she wore a simple yellow nightgown. Her mouth felt full of cotton.

A glass of water sat on the bedside table. She reached for it, but her grip was weaker than she expected, and it slipped from her fingers, splashing water onto the wood.

Kepler woke as it thudded to the floor. He shot to his feet and took her face between his hands. "Ashlyn. You're awake."

His touch was a balm, a comfort. She gave him a weak smile. "I'm thirsty."

"Yes." He turned to the bedside table and did a double take before seeing the glass on the floor. "I'll go get you some water."

He retrieved the glass and left the room.

Alone, Ashlyn looked around again, taking a deep breath. She thought she smelled baking bread, but her senses seemed dull. *My human senses.* She'd never imagined she could miss her wolf so badly. Would Kepler still want to be her mate now? Were they even still bonded? Eyes filming with tears, she sought the mental bond they shared. *Kepler?*

I'm hurrying, love.

She let out a small sob. At least she still had that. She still had a connection.

Ashlyn, what's wrong?

She heard pounding footsteps approaching. *I'm just relieved I can still talk to you this way.*

The footsteps slowed. *Me, too.*

He rounded the doorframe, glass in hand. Tessa and Muffy followed on his heels. He handed Ashlyn the glass of water. "Here."

Ashlyn took a sip, its coolness burning her parched throat. "Thank you."

Tessa came forward carrying a tray with a steaming mug and a plate of toast. She moved to the other side of the bed and set it on the table. "Do you mind if I examine your wound, Ashlyn?"

In a flash, the memory of excruciating pain returned. Cold sweat prickled her skin. She shuddered, sending water sloshing over the rim of her glass.

"Ashlyn?" Kepler steadied her hand with his.

It's okay.

Kepler nodded, and Tessa pulled aside the collar of Ashlyn's nightgown, peeling back the bandage and running cool fingertips over her shoulder blade. "There will be a scar, but I think you're healing nicely."

"How long have I been asleep?" Ashlyn's voice felt scratchy, and she took another sip of water.

"Two days." Kepler tucked a strand of hair behind her ear. "You fought off the agathion for two days."

The last thing she remembered was coming through the hellmouth. "Is it gone?"

"Your aura is fully clear." Tessa smiled. "You're human once more."

The words cut through Ashlyn. *Human.* She slumped back against the pillows. *Not a shifter.*

Kepler pulled his chair close and sat, setting her glass aside to take her hand. "I'm sorry. I know you must be hurting without her."

Tears blurred her eyes, and she nodded.

I'm here for you always. He leaned forward and kissed her forehead. *If I could share my wolf, I would.*

Muffy stepped forward, holding a small animal carrier and looking worried. She glanced at Kepler, then back to Ashlyn. "I have someone who would like to see you, if that's all right?"

Kepler scowled.

Ashlyn looked through the wire door at a small pink nose and striped auburn fur. She sucked in a breath, reaching out. "You made it!"

The lines of worry on Muffy's face softened to relief, and she opened the cage. "This is Hamilton."

The ferret leapt toward Ashlyn, scurrying along to blankets to nuzzle her hands as she stroked his soft fur. He was still bony and light, and the scar over his missing eye looked uncomfortable, but he was no longer matted and dirty.

"God, he stinks," Kepler complained.

Ashlyn frowned. "Be nice. If it wasn't for him, I wouldn't be here. He helped free my wolf so she could..." she choked on the last words. "So she could protect me."

Kepler made a non-committal sound, eyes hard.

She turned back to the ferret. "Thank you, Hamilton, for helping me. I'm glad you escaped." Ashlyn's throat felt tight. She looked back at Muffy. "Why was he there?"

"Hamilton is my sister's familiar. You met her at the bachelorette party. Remember Jen?"

That party felt like it'd happened a million years ago. "I remember Jen, but what's a familiar?"

"Familiars are connected to their witch much the same way a shifter's animal is connected to their human, only we don't swap forms." Muffy set the pet carrier on the floor. "Hamilton went through a hellmouth and got trapped. The agathion held him hostage, forcing Jen to help him."

"That's no excuse." Tessa crossed her arms. "She can never atone for the deaths she caused."

Muffy nodded. "She knows. But she *is* sorry and wanted me to tell you that, Ashlyn." She glanced at Kepler. "She'll tell you personally if you let her."

"Absolutely not," Kepler said.

"Ashlyn, as the only living victim, you have a say in her punishment," Tessa said. "Regardless of whether you wish to speak to Jen or not, she'll be held accountable."

Ashlyn held the ferret a little closer. "What sort of punishment?"

The coven leader looked a little squeamish. "No one has been accused of using this magic in centuries, but the traditional method of execution was death by fire."

Ashlyn had never been a vindictive person, and death by fire seemed barbaric, even for Jen's crimes. "Is there another option?"

"We can find a more humane way for her to die. But her body must be burned in any case. It's the only way to ensure the dark forces she communed with can't use her to return."

Hamilton squeaked and wriggled beneath the covers next to her leg, huddling against her and shivering. Ashlyn took a deep breath. "If Jen dies, what happens to Hamilton?"

"He shares her punishment."

"What?" Her hand fluttered over the shivering lump beneath the covers. "But he was a victim, too!"

"Ashlyn," Kepler said, but she stopped him.

"Can't you strip her of her power or something? There have been enough deaths. All those shifters, now my wolf." A sob caught in her throat.

"Your wolf isn't necessarily dead," Tessa said. "Just disconnected."

Ashlyn sucked in a breath. "What do you mean?"

"Like most spells, shifter magic requires a genetic component to tie this realm with another. The magical energy—in this case, the shifter's animal—is delivered through a constricted channel. Shifters call it the Source. It's a well-guarded portal, allowing only shifter animals through. The hellmouth the agathion used was not guarded and could let anything through. Now we've closed it, you don't have a connection to your wolf."

"So you're saying she could still be alive?"

"Yes."

Ashlyn flung the covers aside. "Kepler, take me to the glacier."

He put a gentle hand on her, keeping her from standing up—which wasn't hard because her legs could barely hold her. "Drinking from the Source a second time will replace your animal."

"But I never drank a first time."

He frowned and looked at Tessa.

She shrugged. "It's shifter magic. I only know the basics."

"I want to try," Ashlyn said.

"The Source may not even open for you."

"We're mates, which means I have an animal—my wolf—waiting for me. I have to go to the Source."

Kepler sighed. "Fine, but I want to do everything right this time. First, we need permission from Councilman Riordan. Let me make a phone call."

Ashlyn nodded and leaned back against the pillows. She'd let Kepler go through shifter channels, at least to start.

But regardless of whether the Council gave permission or not, she was going to the glacier.

Kepler stood on the glacier's surface and waved to the departing helicopter. The pilot saluted and pivoted, taking off toward the cloud-covered sunset. Finch had pulled a lot of strings to let them use the crime unit's helicopter, but Ashlyn had been ready to walk, swim, or crawl to the glacier, even though he'd warned her the Source might not reveal itself.

She slid her mittened hand into his. "Think there'll be an aurora tonight?"

"I hope so." He looked at her, bundled in a down parka and snow bibs, nose pink from the cold. She'd made light of her bulky clothing, pretending she couldn't put her arms down, but he hadn't laughed. Without her animal, she was more susceptible to frostbite and hypothermia than he was. They'd brought a winter tent and a few days of supplies, but if the cave didn't open, he was going to have a hell of a time getting her off this ice.

Even if the cave did open, he hated to think what was going to happen if she ended up with some other animal than her wolf. What if her new animal no longer wanted him as a mate?

As if sensing his worry, she hugged him. "It's going to be fine. My wolf's an Alpha, remember? No way she let that agathion win. She'll find me again."

But the shaking in her voice betrayed her bravado. He wrapped his arms around her, squeezing through all the padding and fluff. "I should be comforting you, not the other way around."

Her lips smiled, but her eyes were tight with concern. "There were other things over there that might want to hurt my wolf."

He'd asked his own wolf what it knew about the other side, but it had been unable or unwilling to provide information. All he could assume was that shifter animals survived there the same way real animals survived in the wilderness. He kissed her forehead. "Like you said, she's an Alpha. She survived among those creatures for who knows how long while she was waiting for her chance to find you."

"That's true." Ashlyn laid her cheek against the front

of his parka. "Besides, I think I'd feel something if she was dead, even if we are disconnected."

He nodded, knowing he'd feel the same way if he lost his wolf.

The cloudy sky had darkened to slate gray, a pale line to the south the only reminder of the setting sun. An icy wind had kicked up, driving snow into his exposed skin and biting through his clothing. If he was chilled, Ashlyn would soon be freezing. "It's going to be full dark soon. Let's set up our tent."

But she refused to release her hold on him. "Kepler, look."

He followed her gaze along the glacier's jagged surface.

Not fifty feet away, a dark hole had opened in the ice.

CHAPTER EIGHTEEN

Ashlyn trembled with excitement and self-doubt. The moment of truth was here. What if her wolf was dead? Worse, what if her wolf *wasn't* dead, and she ended up with another animal? "I'm scared," she whispered.

Kepler's arms tightened around her. "You don't have to do this. We can turn around."

His suggestion that she give up only made her more resolute. "It took me half an hour to put on my snow gear. I'm not chickening out now." She faced the cave and took a deep breath. "Let's do this."

"Wait," he said, digging in a nearby pack. He pulled out their ice cleats. "It may be slippery."

As she pulled the cleats on over her boots, her pulse rushed through her ears and a cold sweat broke out underneath her parka. True darkness had fallen, and with the cloud cover, even the snow looked black. "I can barely see the cave anymore."

"Just follow me."

He squeezed her hand and led her across the jagged ice, their footsteps crunching against the snow. When they reached the entrance, she paused in awe. Deep inside, the ice glowed with faint, blue light. *The same color as my wolf's eyes.* They stepped through, and the color began to flow like water, brightening with hints of yellow and green the deeper they went. Stones littered the cave floor, eventually forming a tunnel leading downward. Deeper and deeper into the ice they went, the living glacier creaking around them.

"This glacier sounds like it's trying to eat us alive," Kepler said, his voice muffled by ice.

She let out a nervous laugh. "This is nothing. You should see the other side of a hellmouth."

Kepler grunted. "Touché."

Eventually, the tunnel opened into a vast cave. The high ceiling danced with shifting ribbons of color more glorious than Ashlyn could've imagined. Trickling water echoed through the space. The cave floor wasn't wet, but it definitely felt warmer than it had outside. Black boulders dotted the ice, some even taller than Kepler. As she crunched toward the cave's center, the glint of falling water caught her eye. From the high ceiling, a thin trickle splattered onto a huge flat stone embedded in the ice.

Ashlyn drew up at the edge. The stone was only a few inches higher than the ice, and the falling water flowed over it to disappear into the glacier beneath. It felt like an altar, of sorts. Definitely otherworldly.

She let out a slow breath and lifted her foot to step onto the stone. "This must be the place."

"Wait," Kepler tugged gently on her hand, pulling her to face him. "A kiss for luck?"

The overhead ice aurora made his eyes glitter with the golden glow of his wolf. Through their mental bond, she sensed his worry. Leaning forward, she pressed her lips softly against his, lingering, savoring the feel of him.

Before she pulled away, he murmured against her, "I love you, Ashlyn Reed. No matter if you get your wolf back, a different wolf, a bear, or nothing at all. You're mine. Always."

She frowned, for the first time considering his stake in her actions. "Are you worried if I get another animal, we'll no longer be mates?"

His lips thinned. "The thought crossed my mind."

"Well, shit. Now I'm worried, too."

"Just don't get a chihuahua for an animal."

She laughed. "Bad jokes are my deal in this relationship, okay?"

One side of his mouth lifted in a smile. "I make no promises."

She gave him one more peck on the lips and

unzipped her parka. It was surprisingly warm inside the cave. "Hold this so I don't get it wet."

"Maybe you should take it all off so you don't ruin your gear if you shift immediately."

She smirked. "You just want to see me naked."

"That, too." He smiled, but his worry still showed through.

Wanting to lighten the mood, she ran her thumbs under the straps of her snow bibs and did a little shimmy as she stripped. "I'm too sexy for these bibs, too sexy for these bibs…"

His laughter echoed through the cave, his gaze following her with a hunger she hoped would remain, whatever the outcome was. Once she was fully naked, she turned back to the water. Goose pimples prickled her skin, and not only because she was naked. What if she did get some weird animal like a chihuahua? *Stop doubting. I'm going to get my wolf back.*

She took a huge breath and leaned toward the waterfall, tilting her head to let the cold liquid fall into her mouth. After several swallows, she stepped back. She didn't feel any different. Her hands looked the same. She still had goose pimples. Then a warm spot spread in her belly. It filled her chest and ran through her limbs.

Overhead, the aurora cracked and snapped, and everything looked clearer. Smelled sharper. Kepler's warm, male scent called to her, filled her with an acute hunger, and she swore she could detect the beating of his heart. As she turned to him, a familiar, joyous howl resonated in her head.

Wolf! Tears blurred her vision. *You're alive! I knew you were stronger than that monster.*

She looked at Kepler, letting her wolf's power rise into her eyes. His worried expression shifted to amazement, then a joy to match her own. "It worked?"

"My wolf is back," her voice choked with a sob.

Whooping, he reached out and swept her into his arms, spinning her once before setting her on her feet and claiming her mouth with his. The mating fire flared within her immediately, and she kissed him fervently, tangling her tongue with his. His parka felt rough against her chest, and she fumbled with the zipper. "You are wearing way too many clothes."

He shucked out of them and yanked her body against his. His thighs were hard against hers, and she lifted one leg up around his hip. He gripped her buttocks with both hands and picked her up the rest of the way, letting her wrap both legs around him. Centered against her core, the length of his erection pulsed with a need that matched her own.

Between kisses, he kicked their snow gear into a pile, then lowered her down toward it. "Oh, no," she said. "This is my party. I'm doing the claiming here."

She gave him a playful shove, and he collapsed onto the nest of parkas, his cock a thick line against his belly. She growled and knelt, wrapping her mouth around it, engulfing him until he hit the back of her throat. He tasted salty and musky and perfect as she cupped his balls and worked his shaft. Groaning, he threaded both hands into her hair, hips bucking upward to meet her with each stroke. "God, woman, you're going to kill me. Come around here so I can taste you."

She swiveled, lifting a knee over his head to straddle him. His tongue flicked out, penetrating her slit, and he grabbed her hips, driving her down against his mouth. He worked her folds as she sucked his shaft until she could no longer concentrate on what she was doing.

Breaking from his hold, she pivoted again, straddling his hips. He bared his teeth, eyes glowing golden, and gripped her ass, helping settle her over his shaft. She was dripping wet, her folds swollen and aching for him. With a solid thrust, she impaled herself on his length, gasping as he filled her, stretched her with exquisite pleasure.

He groaned her name, hips flexing upward to meet her. Her own voice emerged as a growl to match his, "My mate."

"Yes."

Rolling her hips, she started a rhythm, plunging him in and out and ratcheting up the heat growing between them. The tightness in her belly grew and sweat slicked her skin. He moved his hand to press a thumb to her clit, and she exploded, back arching and head thrown back in a scream.

She'd barely finished when he flipped her onto her back and pinned her, continuing his thrusting as his eyes bored into hers.

"Kepler, I'm going to come again." The pressure she'd thought would subside with her first orgasm only rose higher as he drove into her, over and over.

"Mine forever." His teeth had sharpened, and she knew what he meant. What they both needed.

Lifting her mouth to his shoulder, she bit into him the same moment he pierced her skin over the claiming mark he'd made the last time they were together. Lights flashed before her eyes, and a moment of vertigo made her feel as if she'd been thrown back into the hellmouth. Then everything settled, and there was nothing but Kepler. It was as if she could feel his heartbeat inside her own chest.

"I love you, Kepler." She settled back against the arm floor, too spent to move.

Chest heaving, he rested on his elbows above her, one hand stroking her hair as he pressed his forehead against hers. "I love you, too."

When their breathing had settled, he rose and created a nest out of their discarded clothing. Settling her on top of it, he curled up behind her, spooning his warmth against her backside. "Is it wrong I never want to leave here?"

She smiled and wiggled deeper into his embrace,

loving the way his cock pulsed back to life against her ass. "I feel the same way."

Bathed in the blessed light of the Source, they made love the rest of the night.

essa's house was surprisingly silent, considering over twenty people had assembled for Jen's sentencing. Harsh morning sunlight poured through the great room's two-story windows, making everything seem sharper than normal. The plush furniture had been pushed aside, and rows of folding chairs now filled the space. A mix of shifters and witches had divided themselves along an invisible line in each half of the room.

Among the first to arrive, Ashlyn and Kepler sat in front, facing a long table where three Shifter Council members awaited the proceedings. Ashlyn couldn't take her eyes off them. She didn't know why, but she'd expected the shifter leadership to look more like animals. They wore jeans and button-down shirts and had haircuts like any other person she might meet on the street. Sitting beside them, the Head of Covens looked more supernatural than they did, with her perfectly done French knot and flawless tan skin.

Kepler leaned over and whispered in Ashlyn's ear, "Are you certain you want to be here? It's likely to be gruesome."

"Yes, I need to be here. I don't want Hamilton to suffer," Ashlyn said. "And burning Jen alive is barbaric even if Hamilton wasn't included."

"If I could give her worse, I would. She's responsible for the deaths of at least nine shifters, and almost killed you, too."

Ashlyn shook her head. "The agathion did, not Jen."

"She opened the hellmouth," he insisted. "She let him in. She's a liability every second she's alive."

Leveling him with an angry glare, Ashlyn said, "Using that logic, you should've handed me over to the pack and let them kill me."

He had the courtesy to blanch. "I sound just as bad as the pack, don't I?"

She squeezed his hand. "No, but please consider another option besides burning her to death."

Just then, Tessa appeared from a side hallway holding a pet carrier with Hamilton inside. Jen followed a few feet behind her, eyes downcast. Tessa stepped over a small circle of stones that had been placed around a bare wooden chair next to the front table and set the carrier on the floor. Jen sat on the chair and folded her hands in her lap, staring down rather than the assembled crowd. The coven leader stepped away and made a few graceful motions with her hands. Magic prickled through the room, making Ashlyn's skin crawl as though she'd been swarmed by insects.

From the table at the front, the Head of Covens rose. In what had to be an expensive suit and stiletto heels, she looked like she belonged in a New York board room rather than this makeshift trial in the Alaskan outback. "This is the sentencing hearing for Jennifer Lynn Elliot on the matter of using forbidden magic, her part in the deaths of nine shifters, and the endangerment of another. Jennifer has admitted to her crime and agreed to bow to the will of this hearing. Before we proceed, is there anything else the guilty party would like to say?"

Jen looked up, gaze connecting with Ashlyn's for a moment before she dropped it again. "Only that I'm sorry. I never expected people to die, I was trying to save my familiar. It was stupid to fall for the agathion's lies."

"May I speak?" Muffy's voice rose from the crowd.

The Head of Covens frowned, but nodded. "Please provide your name and relationship to the guilty party."

"Muffy, please don't," Jen said as a tear ran down her cheek. "Don't associate yourself with me."

Muffy ignored her. "My name's Muffy and Jen is my sister. I want to point out that what Jen did was a mistake, not intentional. It's like murder one versus manslaughter. I beg the court to consider a reduced sentence."

Councilman Riordan rose from his seat, pale eyes flashing with his wolf's power. "If it happened once, I might call it a mistake. But she let that monster kill those shifters."

"She didn't actually kill them," Muffy pointed out. "In fact, neither did the agathion. They were technically killed by fellow shifters."

The gallery erupted in protest.

"Because they went rogue!"

"Don't try to turn this back on shifters!"

"You don't come back from being rogue."

"Enough!" the Head of Covens said with a forcefulness rivaling any Alpha's.

The audience fell to grumbling silence.

"The point of this hearing is not about the why or how. It is about justice. Jennifer has admitted her guilt. The punishment for her crime is death by fire."

Beside Kepler, Ashlyn rose. "I would also like to speak."

The Head of Coven's eyes twitched in obvious annoyance, but she pursed her mouth and nodded. "It is your right as one of the victims."

"I'm not going to say what Jen did is forgivable, but I do want to point out that her familiar, Hamilton, helped me free my wolf from the agathion's prison. I don't know what part he had in the other shifter's deaths, or why they went rogue while I didn't, but Jen's magic is what saved me in the end. I think Jen and her familiar tried to do the right thing."

"Only because the agathion subverted his promise," Tessa said, her face stony with condemnation.

"What do you mean?" Ashlyn asked, looking between the coven leader and the accused.

More tears slid down Jen's cheek as she stared at the pet carrier where Hamilton had his face against the bars, staring pitifully at Ashlyn. "He promised to free Hamilton after I helped him. He did, only he didn't send Hamilton back to me. Instead, he released my familiar into the hellmouth, alone and unprotected with no way back."

Ashlyn remembered the sensation of being hunted in that dark void and shuddered. She turned to the gallery. "I know I'm a new face here, but I want to advocate for Hamilton. If I understand correctly, a witch's familiar is tied to her in a similar fashion to a shifter's animal." She glanced over her shoulder toward the Head of Covens, who nodded in confirmation. Ashlyn continued, "My wolf was willing to sacrifice herself to save me, and I would do the same for her. I might even be tempted to make rash choices if I thought it would save her. I'm sure all of you feel the same way."

She paused for a heartbeat to allow that idea to sink in before turning back toward the table. "Jen regrets her actions and is willing to pay the price, but burning her alive will also kill Hamilton. Horribly, I might add.

He doesn't deserve that. As one of the victims, I ask that the court consider alternative ways to punish Jen without harming her familiar."

"I understand and appreciate your forgiveness," the Head of Covens said. "But the only way to ensure Jen no longer serves as a conduit for the agathion is the incineration of her soul."

Throat constricted with emotion, Ashlyn asked, "When I came back through the hellmouth, I was able to fight off the agathion's possession by becoming human again. There has to be a way to close off Jen's power and keep the agathion from accessing her, too—besides burning her."

"Yes!" Muffy spoke again, making all heads turn toward her. "Jen can revoke her magic. She can make herself human."

This time it was the witches in the room who gasped. Words like "living death" and "zombie" rumbled through the crowd.

The Head of Covens' cheek twitched as she seemed to consider. "That would break her bond with her familiar. Then he would not suffer her fate."

Jen's already pale face turned ashen. She clenched her hands together on her lap hard enough to make the knuckles gleam white. "If it means Hamilton gets to live, I'll do it."

"And then she won't have to die." Muffy moved toward the front table, looking frantically back and forth between Ashlyn and the Head. "She'll be a harmless human."

"I don't think you understand what you're asking." The Head of Covens frowned deeply. "Such a sentence would only prolong your sister's suffering. She'd most likely kill herself within the first few weeks rather than endure the void of losing her magic."

Ashlyn recalled how devastated she'd been when she lost her wolf. How becoming human again after experiencing the supernatural had hurt. And she had only been connected to her wolf a short time. What would it be like for a witch who'd always possessed power to lose it? "Hold on," Ashlyn looked at Tessa and back to the Head of Covens. "Will that really turn her into a zombie?"

"Not as such, but it will hurt enough to drive her insane," the Head of Covens replied.

Tessa added, "It's a witch's version of going rogue."

Jen leaned forward and set her hand gently on top of the pet carrier. "At least allow me to keep Hamilton from suffering. Afterward you can do as you like to me."

Councilman Dixon, the auburn-haired selkie representative, spoke. "You've been hiding your use of black magic for years. How can we trust you to cast anything, let alone remove your own magic?"

The Head of Covens rubbed her temple and sighed. "I along with several other coven leaders would test her, of course, and verify she had no trace of magic. We would also test her familiar and ensure it reverted to a normal animal. But I'm not recommending this sentence."

Councilman Riordan curled his lips in a very wolfish looking snarl. "I say let her taste her own medicine. Let her suffer what it means to go rogue before she dies."

Ashlyn swallowed, suddenly doubting her part in changing the sentence. Perhaps being burned alive wasn't such a bad option.

The Head of Covens signaled to a witch standing at one side of the room to approach, and whispered something in her ear. The witch disappeared down a hallway, reappearing moments later carrying a small leather pouch, which she handed to the leader. Rising, the Head of Covens approached Jen's chair, her stilettos clicking across the wooden floor. "Please bring out your familiar and rise for your sentence."

With trembling hands, Jen opened the pet carrier and removed Hamilton, lowering her face to press her lips to the top of his head as she stood. When she looked up, her eyes glistened with tears. "We're ready."

"You are hereby sentenced to revoke your magical power immediately and at your own free will, upon which, you will be remanded to your sister's custody for the duration of your life. In the event you do not revoke your power, you will be bound to a stake and burned to ash before the sun rises in the morning. Do you understand?"

Jen nodded, gulping. "Yes."

The Head of Covens opened the leather bag and brought out a small gleaming knife and two tiny vials, one brown, one green. She offered them to Jen.

Hamilton squeaked and squirmed in her arms, burrowing against her neck as if beseeching her to reconsider.

She rubbed her cheek against him one last time before setting him on the floor. "Go, Hamilton."

The little ferret cowered for a moment, looking up at her with his one good eye, then he turned and slunk out of the circle toward Muffy.

Jen took the items, staring stiffly at them for a moment. Then she took a deep breath and made a series of movements with her hands. She emptied the contents of the vials onto the blade, one after the other. Speaking a few shaky words Ashlyn didn't understand, Jen plunged the point beneath her ribs.

Ashlyn gasped as Jen sank slowly to her knees, dropping forward onto one hand while keeping the other clasped around the knife's hilt. A crimson pool grew steadily beneath her, running up to the edge of the circle of stones where it magically stopped. Light pulsed around her as if in time to a beating heart, growing dimmer with each flash until it vanished.

Taking a step forward, Ashlyn was going to try to stop the bleeding, but Kepler's grip on her arm stopped her. "Don't interfere."

She watched in horror as Jen yanked the knife free

and sagged onto her side, curling into a fetal position. The knife fell from her hand into the pooling blood, it's once-gleaming metal now corroded and black.

"Is she dead?" Ashlyn whispered.

The witches in the gallery rose in a whoosh of sound and approached the circle of stones. Forming a solid wall, they faced the circle, and a hum of magic filled Ashlyn's ears, encircling her heart until she could hardly breathe. She glanced at Muffy, who held Hamilton against her chest, tears glistening on her reddened cheeks. The ferret squirmed and writhed, but Muffy held on tightly.

Suddenly, the magic ceased, and the wall of witches parted. Jen lay where she'd fallen, shoulders shaking with silent sobs. The blood on the floor had vanished. Hamilton escaped Muffy's grasp, scurrying under the chairs and disappearing from sight.

The Head of Covens addressed the room. "It is done. Let it be known that the covens have verified that Jennifer Lynn Elliot has revoked her magic and is now a mortal human. She is no longer under the protection of our order."

A chorus of "Aye" rose from the witches, along with a few disgruntled words from the assembled shifters.

Councilman Riordan stood, his piercing gaze silencing the crowd. "The witch has served her sentence. Although she no longer falls under the protection of the witches, be warned that anyone who harms her will be held accountable for harming a human without cause."

The shifters in the gallery muttered their reluctant acceptance of his announcement. Ashlyn got the feeling Jen might not have long to live, anyway. Muffy was on her knees next to her sister, encouraging her to stand. Although Jen's eyes were open and her chest moved with rapid breaths, there was a deadness to her gaze that Ashlyn recognized. She'd felt it herself when she lost her wolf.

She almost felt sorry for the witch.

Almost.

Kepler leaned against the countertop and sipped his coffee, watching Ashlyn as she moved around the bakery kitchen with her cousin, Lana. He needed to get to work, but hated leaving his mate's side for even a few hours after everything they'd been through. Plus, she fed him muffins when he came to the bakery, so he spent his mornings there before going to the office.

Lana hefted a tray of doughnuts and carried it to the front customer area, shoving it into the glass case near the register before returning to the kitchen. He liked Ashlyn's cousin, but she put a bit of a damper on his ability to be frisky with his new mate. She kept glancing out the front windows, and he had the feeling there was more to her hanging around the bakery these last few days than having her boat dry-docked for repairs.

The bell over the door jingled, and Cal's voice carried into the kitchen. "It's just me!"

Lana's face brightened, and she tucked a loose strand of unruly blonde hair under her baseball cap before rearranging the bear claws on a tray for what had to be the dozenth time.

Kepler shot a glance at Ashlyn, raising one eyebrow in an "I told you so," fashion.

Ashlyn's eyes twinkled, and she sent, *She has a crush.*

It can't go anywhere. He shook his head. *She's not his mate, or he would've said something.*

Her face fell. *Crap.* Lana had lost her husband a while back, and Ashlyn was super protective of her.

Cal strutted into the kitchen wearing his new brown Wildlife Trooper uniform. After the hearing, Finch had finagled Cal an entry level position. Kepler'd never seen his friend this happy.

Glancing at Kepler's maroon tee shirt as he bee-lined it toward the bear claws, Cal said, "Nice shirt, man."

"Thanks," Kepler replied. The shirt said *stop looking at my wife's cookies*, and Ashlyn had giggled about it for hours after he'd put it on it.

Cal nodded at Lana as he helped himself to a pastry. "Hey, how's it going?" Without waiting for her reply, he pulled a stool out and sat facing Kepler. "So, you decide yet?"

Lana's cheeks flushed, and she dusted imaginary flour off her jeans. "Um, yeah, good. I'm good. I need to go."

She rushed out of the kitchen and through the front door, the cold smell of snow driving away the smell of baked goods for a moment.

Ashlyn frowned. "What was that all about?"

Cal looked just as confused, speaking around a mouthful of bear claw. "No idea. I thought we had a good time last night."

Kepler narrowed his eyes and stared his friend down. "You didn't."

"What? Yeah, we did." He polished off the bear claw.

Throwing her oven mitt aside, Ashlyn peeked into the customer area before rounding on Cal. "You shouldn't lead her on."

"I'm not. She came over last night to chill, you know?" He shrugged.

Kepler set his coffee aside and put his hands on his hips. Shifters often dallied with humans on a casual basis, knowing it wouldn't lead to anything permanent. But Kepler'd never really thought about how a human might hope differently. "Lana is off limits."

Cal frowned. "She's a grown woman. She's got needs the same as the rest of us."

"She's fragile, Cal." Ashlyn sighed. "Just leave her alone, okay?"

Cal's face fell, and he nodded. "Fine." He reached for a second bear claw. "But we did have fun."

Ashlyn smacked his hand with a scowl. "Paws off the claws. Those are for customers."

"I like it better when Lana's in charge." He licked his fingers. "Don't I at least get a pack discount or something?"

Cal had been bugging him since the honeymoon to register their new pack with the Council, but Kepler wasn't sure he was ready. He was still focused on spending time with Ashlyn. "Stop bugging me about the pack thing. I haven't decided."

"Let Ashlyn do it. She's as Alpha as you are." Cal licked his finger and used it to pick up crumbs from an empty baking tray. "More Alpha, maybe."

Ashlyn's scowl dissolved into a smirk. "Kepler's right about you being a suck up, Cal." She shook her head. "But I kinda like it."

Cal grinned in triumph. "See, Kep? Listen to your better half." He snagged a bear claw and scooted past Ashlyn before she could stop him. "Gotta go. Finch wants me to find out who's been harassing moose around Skilak Lake. See ya!"

Kepler looked at his phone. It was seven thirty. "I should go, too."

Ashlyn put a hand on his chest. "We really should talk."

He sighed. She was less opposed to forming a pack than he was. Covering her hand with his, he looked into her eyes. "It's a tremendous responsibility."

She wrapped her other arm around his waist, tilting

her head to look up at him. "Cal's a worthy pack mate, even if he is a pastry thief. It's good to have friends who'll watch your back."

He hated to admit it, but she was right. Cal had pulled through for him, even when he'd doubted. "What about Finch?"

She made a confused face. "Isn't it weird for a bear to join a pack?"

"My point exactly. And Finch is my boss. How's it going to work if I'm his Alpha?"

Her eyes narrowed to crescents as she grinned. "You get to tell him to give you a raise, I guess."

He laughed. "Always the jokes."

"You thought I was joking?" She raised her eyebrows. "Seriously, though, it'll all work out. I know it will. And we'll all live happily ever after."

Pulling her closer, he inhaled her wildflower honey scent. "I already am."

He'd never imagined feeling this content. He'd found his mate, nearly lost her, and got her back stronger than ever. Lowering his head, he kissed her, savoring her taste and softness. By the time they stopped, he was breathing hard and ready to plunder her right there.

She nuzzled his chin, a naughty grin lighting her glowing blue eyes. "Go to work, my love. But don't wear yourself out. I have plans for you tonight."

He grinned and kissed her forehead. They had years together—centuries. And he could hardly wait.

Dear Reader,

Thank you for reading Kepler and Ashlyn's story! I enjoyed bringing the paranormal to Alaska. Be sure to check out the other books in the Alaska Alpha series. You can find them all here:

< https://books2read.com/rl/aurorashifters >

More to come in the series this summer! While you wait, you may also like my Mates for Monsters series, with hot shapeshifting mermen, steamy centaur cowboys, and even a book featuring the agathion's evil djinn cousins! (The Djinn's Desire) Go read it now!

XOXO
Tamsin

Galactic Pirate Brides series

Rescued by Qaiyaan

Ransomed by Kashatok

Claimed by Noatak

Mates for Monsters

Mer-Lovers Illustrated Collector's Edition

The Merman's Kiss

The Merman's Quest

A Mermaid's Heart

The Centaur's Bride

The Djinn's Desire

Khargals of Duras

Sticks and Stones

Alaska Alphas

Alpha Origins

Untamed Instinct

Bewitched Shifter

ABOUT AURORA SHIFTERS

Aurora Shifters is a collaboration of Alaskan authors who decided to put our own Arctic spin on hot paranormal shapeshifters.

Tielle St. Clare moved to Alaska when she was seven years old and believes romances should be hot and sexy with a great story and fun characters. Learn more about her at www.tiellestclare.blogspot.com

Tamsin Ley was born and raised in Alaska and writes steamy sci-fi with a pinch of pixie dust. Find out more about her at www.tamsinley.com

Boone Brux has lived all over the world, finally settling in the icy region of Alaska. No person or escapade is off limits when it comes to weaving real life experiences into her books. Learn more at www.boonebrux.com

Be sure to join the Alaska Alphas Facebook Group! www.facebook.com/groups/alaskaalphas/

facebook.com/AlaskaAlphas
bookbub.com/authors/aurora-shifters
amazon.com/author/aurorashifters